THE FINAL ENEMY

Also by Alanna Knight

THE FINAL ENEMY

An Inspector Faro Mystery

Alanna Knight

BLACK & WHITE PUBLISHING

First published 2002
by Black & White Publishing Ltd
99 Giles Street, Edinburgh EH6 6BZ

ISBN 1 902927 28 1

Typeset by Hewer Text Ltd, Edinburgh
Printed and bound by Creative Print and Design, Ebbw Vale, Wales

To Campbell, Suzy, Benjamin and grandpa Pierre

'For he must reign,
till he hath put all enemies under his feet.
The last enemy that shall be destroyed is death.'

1 Corinthians

1

'ATTEMPTED ASSASSINATION AT KAISER'S HUNTING-LODGE' ran the headline.

In smaller print: 'Her Majesty the Queen who is the Kaiser Wilhelm's grandmother is deeply distressed by the news . . .'

In the garden of 9 Sheridan Place, the newspaper lay unread on the grass. It did not merit a second glance from Jeremy Faro, recently retired as Chief Inspector of Edinburgh City Police.

The 1880s had been notable for attempts on royal personages. Scandals and assassinations were fashionable as were highly lucrative pursuits of international villains who found times of political unrest greatly to their advantage.

The Russian Emperor had been blown to pieces by nihilists, and across the Atlantic President Garfield had fallen victim to an assassin's bullet.

Earlier that year, in January 1889, the courts of Europe had been shocked by news that the Crown Prince of Austria-Hungary, only son and heir of Emperor Franz Joseph, had committed suicide after shooting his eighteen-year-old mistress in the hunting-lodge at Mayerling.

'I have your queen. I have killed her!'

A shrill voice at his side and Faro shuddered. The past decade had also been notable for several attempts, all carefully hushed-up, on Her Majesty's life, frustrated by the speedy intervention of Inspector Jeremy Faro.

Had he been tempted by the newspaper fluttering in the gentle breeze, it would have been to sigh with relief that such matters were no longer any of his business or responsibility. His greatest concern at the present moment was averting a more imminent domestic disaster.

Another shrill cry. 'Look, I have killed your queen, Grandpa.'

Faro sighed and glanced at the chessboard. To his cost he had been teaching five-year-old Jamie to play. An apt pupil, though with a regrettable tendency to cheat. This was currently demonstrated by driving his black knight straight across the board regardless of any rules, ruthlessly belting the white queen such a mortal blow that she toppled on to the grass and came to rest in very unseemly royal fashion beside the unread newspaper.

Again Faro sighed. 'Pick her up if you please, Jamie. And the correct term is "checkmate" not "kill".'

Jamie grinned, an endearing mass of yellow curls and guileless blue eyes. 'But I won, didn't I, Grandpa? I polished her off,' he said triumphantly. 'And that is what counts.'

Leaping from his seat, he put his arms around his step-grandfather's neck and hugged him. 'That is one crime you needn't bother to solve, is it not?'

'Indeed it is not. Thank you for that, Jamie,' said Faro drily.

In truth he had no more crimes to solve ever and that pleased him exceedingly. Death and disaster on such a day as this seemed mere flights of fancy, a far cry from his peaceful garden watched over by the long extinct volcano famous as Arthur's Seat.

He sighed happily, from this oasis of joy with a beloved family, content in the knowledge that there would be many other days just as good. Peaceful days that would stretch into his sunset years . . .

Again he sighed. At the certainty of a blissful, uneventful life stretching into a future, infinitely preferable to putting up with, and putting his life at risk from, the criminal fraternity.

Replacing the chessmen on the board for the umpteenth time, he smiled. 'We'll try again, shall we, Jamie?'

The only threat to that warm late October day had been a white queen at risk from Jamie's passionate disregard for the rules of the game. The only cloud on his day was a talk to be given on Founder's Day at Glenatholl College. The future had approached with alarming rapidity, to become 'tomorrow'.

It hampered his spirit like an undigested meal, regarded with considerably more anxiety than facing any villain.

This tranquil scene in the garden was overlooked by Jamie's father, Dr Vince Laurie, writing at his open study window. With feelings relaxed and paternal he observed his pretty young wife Olivia taking off the heads of the last summer roses.

Under shady trees the latest addition to the family, their brand-new daughter, lay in her perambulator and Vince hoped that she would remain inert for a while longer and that peace would continue to reign over the household.

He shook his head in wonderment. In all his years of handling new-born infants he had never heard such a monstrous loud voice issuing forth from a mere six pounds of humanity. It was, he firmly believed, quite capable of shattering crystal and he winced at Jamie's shrill cry, certain it would wake that small volcano of sound.

His son hated to lose, loved this new game, the feeling of infinite power of moving kings, queens, bishops and knights across a chessboard. Laying aside his medical books, Vince went down the stairs and into the garden.

With an arm around Jamie, he said to Faro. 'This one is going to be a politician, I fear, Stepfather. And that will break his dear mother's heart. She has already pinned her hopes on a doctor or an artist.'

He had spoken loud enough for Olivia to overhear. Laying aside the secateurs, she tiptoed over to the sleeping babe and, ignoring Vince's remarks, said sternly 'You mustn't cheat, Jamie – that's very naughty. Gentlemen don't cheat.'

'Are you including doctors and artists in that category, my dear?' teased Vince and to Faro. 'He has picked up chess amazingly – better than I did when you tried to teach me as a wee lad.'

Faro smiled at the memory, albeit a little painfully since he had been singularly unsuccessful in that respect with the sullen resentful stepson who had been eight-year-old Vince.

Now joining the trio gazing fondly upon the new arrival, he was relieved that Olivia's pregnancy was safely over, remembering all too well the hazards that had taken Vince's mother, his own beloved Lizzie. Two girls, Rose and Emily, then a stillborn son had cost her her life and brought Vince and Faro with less than twenty years between them close as brothers in their shared grief.

Such were the thoughts in Faro's mind surrounded by that scene of happy family life. Ruffling Jamie's curls, so like his father's in boyhood, he said:

'Aye, I reckon you'll be like all little lads, won't you. First you'll be a lamplighter and go through all the stages to lord advocate. Then perhaps you'll please your mamma by settling for a respectable Edinburgh profession.'

'And Baby must be an opera singer with a voice like that,' said Vince.

Their laughter was accompanied by a blackbird's bitter-sweet requiem to a dying year, although on that radiant afternoon, cruel winter and such melancholy intimations were not even visible as a tiny dark cloud to mar an azure sky.

The kitchen door opened and there was Mrs Brook, bringing out a tea tray. Vince leapt up to assist her. Jamie followed suit, rushing forward to be restrained from seizing a piece of her excellent sponge cake.

As he wailed that he loved Mrs Brook's cakes, she smiled indulgently on these dear people she had served as housekeeper for many years and come to regard not as employers, but as her family.

Dr Laurie now occupied the whole house, his surgery shared with a medical partner. Two rooms were set aside for guests and his father's fleeting visits, on the first floor were the family apartments, and above were attics, the domain of a nanny and a maid. Mrs Brook had been reluctantly persuaded by increasing age and a certain stiffness in her joints, which she refused to admit, plus the doctor's increasing family, that she could no longer take care of the whole house single-handed.

Sipping his tea, Faro sat back in his chair. So this was retirement. He sighed blissfully, happy and at peace with the world.

Vince took the seat opposite and had stretched out his hand for the still-folded newspaper with its sensational headline, when a noise like a foghorn, or a ship in distress on the distant River Forth signalled that Baby, as she was presently known, was awake.

The fond father leaped to his feet and rushed over to the perambulator. 'Baby – hello – a smile for your Pappa.'

Baby indeed, thought Faro, she had not yet a name and would continue her anonymous existence until her parents made the difficult choice. A decision which threatened to wreck that otherwise happy marriage. Vince wanted Mary or Elizabeth (Lizzie after his mother) while Olivia wanted Amelia after her own grandmother. Daily the argument continued back and forth and as the time of registration loomed, unheeded, it seemed that Miss Laurie would be doomed to be known as Baby for the rest of her life.

Faro, asked to mediate, said tactfully he thought Mary more appropriate. Without the merest flicker of presentiment he had his own uncomfortable reasons for not wanting a granddaughter called Amelia.*

* *The Missing Duchess* (Macmillan 1994)

Some thirteen years ago he had known an Amelie, the foreign version of Amelia. She rarely entered his thoughts any more and he had little desire to have a constant daily reminder of that thoroughly unsettling incident, – a strange mystery and the brief emotional turmoil which had marked his encounter with the Grand Duchess of Luxoria.

Such matters were past history, voluntary retirement had settled dangerous royal rescues for ever. Here was peace at last, he told himself very frequently – the time he had waited for, scarred by thirty years of dealing with the threat of death.

Here was the Indian summer of a man's life. Content, he lolled in a garden chair, with a pile of unread books at his side and an unwritten lecture for Glenatholl College the only serpent in his Eden.

When that was over, he could indulge again his newly found love of travel. The excitement of new places in Europe had been denied him during his long service, which included serving Her Majesty incognito as personal detective within limits set by the Borders of England and Scotland. Now the popularity of rail travel, of frequent trains at home and on the Continent, opened up new opportunities for fast and comfortable travel.

At his side, Vince, setting down his teacup, picked up the newspaper and about to open it, folded it once again in an irritable gesture as the sudden breeze threatened to wrest it from his grasp. Seeing Olivia carrying Baby into the house for her afternoon feed, he said, 'Can't read outside – think I'll go in. Come along, Jamie. Grandpa has work to do.'

Faro smiled. 'Let him stay.'

'If he promises to be good. How's the talk for Glenatholl coming along?'

'Where's Glen-ath-oll? Can I come?' demanded Jamie.

'Not this time, but some day when you are older, you will be going there as a pupil. You'll like that,' said Vince.

'Is it far? And will Baby be going too?'

'It isn't very far, and no, Baby won't be going. It's a boys' public school.'

Famous too. And costly since most of the crowned heads of Europe and Asia, and the world's wealthiest and mightiest, sent their sons there to be educated. Without barrier of colour or creed, Glenatholl prided itself on liberalism, or more candidly, the production of a reliable bank account by parent or guardian.

Faro remembered how he had paid for Vince's education after Lizzie died, saving and scrimping on a policeman's salary to send him to university. To be a doctor. Now, unless Vince achieved his ambition of becoming Queen's physician, his long-dreamed-of ambition, he was unlikely to be able to afford his son's fees at Glenatholl.

Though Vince was delighted when his stepfather had been chosen to give the Founder's Day lecture, Faro, alas, did not share his enthusiasm. Regarding the event with growing dread, he would have liked to find a suitable excuse to refuse, but was unable to do so without sounding churlish, as well as wounding Vince's hopes for Jamie.

In truth his talk was at present only a few notes on the back of an envelope. He felt totally unable to put his thoughts down on paper and read them aloud and, more importantly, was unsure whether his choice of lecture subject would be compelling to the boys. 'Crime', yes, but 'In Our Society'? How could he hope to stimulate the interest or arouse the sympathy of such pupils for the appalling conditions of Edinburgh's poor and the crimes it nurtured? It would be a foreign field indeed for these sons of the rich and noble in their cushioned existence. However, he would tell them interesting anecdotes and hope that no one fell asleep, or had to be excused feeling sick.

'You'll have Arles Castle to look forward to after your talk, Stepfather. Perth should be looking marvellous if this weather holds and it must be – how many years since you last saw Sir Julian? Before he remarried, wasn't it? And there's now a son and heir. What a relief that must be for him after all those childless years.'

Sir Julian's first wife, to whom he had been devoted, had long been an invalid. Faro had been at her funeral four years ago.

'The break will do you a power of good,' Vince continued in his best doctor-patient voice, following Olivia and Baby into the house and clutching under his arm that instrument of his stepfather's nemesis, the daily newspaper.

2

Idly watching his stepfather from the kitchen window while Olivia, having given Nanny the day off, prepared Miss Laurie for her afternoon feed, Vince considered the man and the small boy, their heads bent over the chessboard in a garden tinged with the reds, golds and purple of a perfect autumn day.

The still-handsome man, the Viking from Orkney, the tarnished fair hair becomingly streaked with silver. The strange long eyes, deep blue and piercing, slightly hooded like a bird of prey. The delicately hooked straight nose and full mouth.

Olivia came to his side and interpreted his thoughts as she often did. 'He doesn't look past fifty, does he?'

'Indeed he does not,' and Vince ruefully touched his own thinning hair, once a mass of thick curls like Jamie's.

'Put a helmet with horns on him and he'd still look as if he'd stepped off a Viking ship,' said Olivia.

'And strike terror into the hearts of all the womenfolk,' said her husband.

'Oh I don't know about that, dearest,' was the smooth response, 'there should be worse fates than being carried off by such an attractive man.'

Vince chuckled. 'My darling, you read too many romances.'

Olivia sighed. 'I wish he'd read more romances.'

Her husband looked at her quickly. 'Marry again, is that what you have in mind? Perhaps this visit to Sir Julian will put him in the right frame of mind. After all, he's older than Stepfather.'

'Not marry again in general, I don't mean that. Just marry Imogen. She's so right for him, Vince.'

'It isn't for lack of trying on his part, reading between the lines I think it is what he most wants. Not that Imogen would make the perfect wife. She isn't a county type, like Lady Arles. And I can't see Imogen settling down to an Edinburgh social life of luncheons and dinners and calling cards. Now, can you? Admit it!'

Olivia sighed again and shook her head. 'Not even remotely, dear. Still one of the wild Irish, I suppose.'

'And no bad thing,' said Vince loyally. 'Anyway, Stepfather and Imogen are happy as they are. What's wrong with that?'

'It's so – unconventional. I don't know how to introduce her – '

'Luckily there aren't too many occasions,' said Vince drily, refraining from adding what Olivia clearly knew only too well from her 'wild Irish' remark – that Imogen was still in danger under British law, classed as a wanted Fenian terrorist. Although it had never been proved, she was wise to travel incognito.

She showed wisdom in not wishing to become Faro's wife in the eyes of the law and knowing Imogen, Vince decided that she remained his companion only – whatever happened when the bedroom door was closed – in Faro's own interests and for his good reputation's sake. Imogen Crowe might have reformed but Vince did not doubt that there were many who would have seized any opportunity to throw her into prison.

'You're quite right, dear, of course,' said Olivia. 'There are many problems they have to face. But relationships like theirs are a little, well – untidy, you must admit.'

Considering that the highest in the land, namely the Prince of Wales himself, had set a fashion in mistresses, Vince did not feel that his stepfather's reputation would sustain any lasting damage.

And as Olivia carried Baby up to the nursery to feed her, followed by Mrs Brook with the week's meals to discuss, his eyes drifted once more to that scene in the garden below. A moment he wished he could capture for eternity, one to take out and regard in wonder over the coming years.

He shivered, his normally practical soul disturbed by a strange feeling that it was vital to halt time's relentless progress. To preserve in amber this scene of a man and a boy, heads bent over a chessboard.

Olivia was a talented amateur painter and hearing her talking to Mrs Brook, he thought this was what she should be doing instead of concerning herself with dreary matters of no importance whatever, such as whether it should be roast beef or lamb on the menu.

He shook his head, unfolded the newspaper and turned to the back page in search of the most important item – the results of the golfing championship at St Andrews' famous 'Royal and Ancient' course.

Meanwhile, unaware that his relationship with Imogen Crowe had been the subject of such speculation, Faro stretched out his hand to the pile of books beside him and selected one more challenge he had set himself – a foreign language to be speedily learned, or so *German in Six Easy Lessons* implied. It would be a useful and necessary addition for his travels in Europe at the side of the Irish writer, his devoted friend and companion, as he described her.

He would very much have liked to change all that and make her his wife, but Imogen would have none of it. She had been free too long and, in her early forties, she considered herself too old to have children even if she had wanted them.

Imogen had a suffragette's attitude to marriage, to any threats to women's freedom for which she had fought so long. And Faro loved her independence, her wit and humour, her passionate dedication to the world's lost causes, although he failed entirely to convince her that he might be eligible for inclusion as a failed suitor. And most of all there was Ireland, her dedication to Home Rule, for which she had sacrificed much in the past, including members of her family murdered for their patriotism.

So Faro followed her to France, to Italy, Austria and Germany, where he found himself for the first time at a considerable disadvantage. Unable to understand a word being said around him, he lurked in the background, a polite observer with a fixed smile, until Imogen, a natural linguist, became aware of his discomfort and embarrassment and patiently translated for him. This was a situation to be deplored, it annoyed him intensely and he made a stern resolve to put his retirement to good use.

Having been constantly shamed and outraged by the British abroad, who believed that if they shouted loud enough in English, their wishes could be understood and instantly obeyed, he determined that, as a prospective traveller in foreign parts, he would courteously learn to communicate with his hosts.

At a recent dinner party in Sheridan Place, he mentioned the problem of learning German to a golfing friend of Vince's who was also Professor of Languages at the University. Immediately interested, since everyone who was anyone, he said, knew of Faro's fame as Scotland's most senior detective, the professor assured him that if he liked solving mysteries then language was a particularly daunting one.

'You have to have a natural ear, a natural aptitude. But perhaps I can help you with some short cuts. I have a couple of hours free on a Wednesday afternoon. Perhaps, if I may offer you the benefits of my experience – '

Faro had been delighted. At this precise moment while he sat in his Edinburgh garden enjoying the autumn sunshine, Imogen would be in Munich, heading for Heidelberg University where she was to meet other Irish exiles, writers and artists, who had introduced her to a new passion – Wagnerian opera.

She enthused in recent letters about Lisa, a new German friend and a diva. 'A wonderful Isolde with a life almost as tragic. You must meet her.' That pleasant thought spurred on his determination to learn *hoch Deutsch* – high German, the accepted tongue for the circles Imogen travelled in.

Faro loved to surprise Imogen, wanting her to be impressed by his perseverance and efficiency, confident that by their next meeting he would have solved his most baffling mystery at present – the basics of German grammar. Once he had cracked that code, he felt, he would be well on the way to success, and he had to admit that this new challenge of mastering language was very exhilarating.

The pronounciation texts at their weekly meetings required considerable concentration from Faro, but the Professor was pleasantly surprised by his new pupil's dexterity.

'Languages,' he had firmly maintained and warned Faro at that first meeting, 'are best learned when one is young.'

He had had to change his ideas, however, for although it was still early days to expect Faro's abilities to stretch to philosophical conversation, his accent and understanding were outstanding. 'Here is a man in his fifties,' he told his friends, 'a better and more apt pupil than many of my young and eager students.'

German in Six Easy Lessons. Chapter Four.

Suddenly the blackbird's eulogy was interrupted by Jamie's triumphant shout.

'I've killed your queen. Again, Grandpa. Bang – she's dead.'

Faro's concentration had been distracted while he closed his eyes and tried to memorise a particularly tricky nominative clause.

Now Jamie, with a cavalier disregard for rules, was lolloping his black bishop across the board.

'Checkmate, Jamie,' Faro repeated patiently. 'Checkmate, remember. That's what we call it. Not kill!'

He turned back to Chapter Four. The blackbird had flown away and all was silent. He was at peace with his world.

But not for very much longer.

That tiny unseen black cloud on the horizon was growing steadily larger and threatening to destroy everything. In the shape of Vince it was hurtling across the garden towards him. The bright day was over and life itself would never be the same again.

'Stepfather!' Vince was in front of him, flourishing the newspaper. 'Stepfather, have you seen this?'

Bewildered, Faro shook his head and Vince said: 'I've just read it. This assassination business in Mosheim. Listen, "An attempt has been made on the life of the Grand Duchess of Luxoria, the Kaiser's guest at his autumn shooting-party. Her equerry took the first bullet trying to save his mistress and died instantly. One of the Kaiser's guards was also fatally wounded." '

Vince took a deep breath. 'There's a bit more, "Her Majesty the Queen is gravely concerned about the condition of the Grand Duchess, who is her goddaughter, as well as any danger threatening her favourite grandson, Kaiser Wilhelm.'

Faro had gone suddenly cold, vaguely remembering seeing the headline as it had lain idly within reach while he and Jamie played chess. If it had aroused any feelings at all, they would have been of congratulating himself that this was one royal murder plot that was no concern of his.

But Amelie . . . Amelie.

Memory rewarded him with a vision of her sleeping head on the pillow beside him while a storm raged beyond the bedroom window. His bedroom window, visible here from the garden.

He took the newspaper from Vince, hardly daring to read. The words swam before his eyes and Vince noticed that emotion made Faro's hand tremble.

He had tried to abolish Amelie from his thoughts over the years, but the possibility of the new baby in Sheridan Place being given the same name had touched a core of unease.

He had told himself long ago that his brief role in her life was over. By mutual consent the line had been drawn under it. Now old feelings awakened. How would he feel if she were already dead?

His mind sped back over the years. Back thirteen years to the brief wild passion and the official announcement of the royal prince's birth. 'After many years of marriage to President Gustav of Luxoria, Her Highness the Grand Duchess Amelie has given birth to an heir. Born prematurely, despite fears for his survival, the prince shows every sign of being a strong, healthy infant.'

A week later, Faro had received a letter with a Luxorian stamp. It contained a copy of the announcement and underneath in ink, the cryptic words, 'We have a son.'

No further information arrived, no further communication across the years. Nor did he want any more than that. The child had saved her life from the President who had already attempted to kill her for having failed to produce an heir, determined to usurp the throne and have his mistress and his natural son installed. A child was vital to save the kingdom and Amelie's life.

Faro could count as well as the next man but he had never told anyone of his suspicions concerning the child's conception, although he often thought that Vince knew and was troubled by the possible consequences of that brief interlude.

For years now it had only remained for Faro to convince himself he had misunderstood Amelie's cryptic message, sent only to reassure him that she was still alive, safe and well.

As time passed he began to believe it.

He had never told Imogen.

3

Monday afternoon and had Faro any reason for gratitude, it was to the work on his lecture, which had needed all his powers of concentration. Fortunately it had also kept his mind from dwelling on the bombshell Vince and the newspaper had dropped on his life that Sunday afternoon.

Now, as the train steamed across the Perthshire countryside carrying him in the direction of Glenatholl College, he was again haunted by nightmare and indecision, remembering another train journey, across Europe with Imogen.

They had been close to the Luxorian border and Faro had shown a firm reluctance to visit a writer of Imogen's acquaintance who was living in the capital. Accompanying her never failed to reveal an unlimited swarm of exiled Irish writers and displaced artists, a world-wide fraternity of which Imogen, it seemed, knew every one.

How would she react to the outcome of a romantic encounter, too brief to be dignified as a love affair, he wondered anxiously. Would she even care, used as she was in her dealings with the suffrage of women to the less conventional aspects of a Bohemian life? Would she be sympathetic to a child whom he could never acknowledge as his own?

There was no action he could take. He was helpless to do more than watch and wait for the official newspaper reports, no easy task for a man used to swift decisive action all his life. If only he could travel to the Odenwald, find out for himself – there was always the excuse of Imogen as far as Vince and Olivia were concerned.

Had it been Luxoria he would have been tempted to leave on the next available train, throw caution to the winds. But that was hardly sensible. His German wasn't up to it yet, regardless of Amelie's insistence that Luxoria was very Anglophile, a common factor shared by many minority European states with close kinship to Queen Victoria and Prince Albert. According to Amelie, almost everyone – by that he had guessed she was referring to the upper classes and court circles – spoke fluent English.

Faro was not convinced. His long association with the Edinburgh City Police had developed in him instinctive faculties of caution and tact in dealing with difficult and dangerous situations, particularly regarding impulsive action where personal emotions were involved.

Besides, his hands were effectively tied until after Glenatholl and his visit to Arles Castle. He regarded the latter in a hopeful light, not merely as an opportunity to renew an old acquaintance. Since Sir Julian had been an ambassador in various European courts, perhaps it would yield significant information about Luxoria.

'Perth!' shouted the guard.

Faro strolled along the platform with his overnight valise. He had declined the offer of being met by the Glenatholl carriage at the railway station. There were always hiring cabs at railway stations, he had assured them. At least, such was the case in Edinburgh. Or was he being strictly honest? Was he merely delaying the moment of arrival at the college, of stepping down into a vast array of masters and pupils eagerly awaiting a famous man's arrival?

He did not want that. More than ever he needed time to himself, to think over his talk and plan his next move. All his life, in times of crisis he had learned the value of his own society, of retreating into his own thoughts. Although he sometimes found it difficult to convince his family, and his two daughters in particular, that being solitary was not the same as being alone.

Yes, it had been a good idea to keep his train's arrival time to himself, he decided, sitting back to enjoy the glory of a perfect autumn day and surprising the cab driver with his request to be put down at the college gates.

'It's a fair step, mister, a mile or more,' the driver said, looking his 'fare' over with the gimlet eye of long experience. 'Another sixpence will see you to the very door.'

In appearance every indication of a gentleman, smartly dressed and carrying hand luggage, this particular fare might not be able to afford another sixpence. However, in the driver's experience well-to-do travellers were the most ready to niggle over a few extra coppers.

He looked slightly confused when he realised from Faro's shrewd expression that his thoughts had been rightly interpreted.

'I like to walk, cabbie. And it's a fine afternoon for it.'

'As you wish, mister.'

The entrance to Glenatholl was marked by a handsome lodge and a winding drive of rhododendrons. A riot of colour in summer, no doubt, but now flowerless, the unmoving mass of dark impenetrable green appeared gloomy and somewhat forbidding.

Faro consulted his watch. Still almost an hour before he was due to give his talk. Time for a little exercise, time to breathe and stretch his long legs. Time, also, for that last invaluable glance at his notes, to commit as much as possible to memory.

He hated the idea of standing at a lectern reading his almost illegible writing and he hated wearing the eyeglasses he needed for such tasks these days. It wasn't so much pride, the threat of increasing age and its devastation on such faculties, he could deal with that, but he had a natural abhorrence of relying on anything, however trifling, that threatened his independence. And eyeglasses he regarded as such, a crutch for use *in extremis*, a weakness not yet for public exhibition.

As he walked, the heavy green bushes opened into a vista of archery course and playing fields where boys were playing out of season cricket, doubtless using the time for valuable practice.

Beyond the fields arose the turrets and roof of the college. Across an expanse of turf near at hand was a walled garden. Hoping to find a seat for his meditations, Faro found the gate open and was soon making his way down a terrace flanked by stern-visaged toga-clad Roman senators.

Excellent! The right company for one making a speech he decided, walking between the two lines of statues to a gazebo in keeping with the style of ancient Rome overlooking an artificial lake. The swans on the lake, although the same ghostly white as the senators, were at least living and watched his approach with curiosity. Bathed in sunshine, the gazebo's stone benches would provide a tolerably warm place with enough light to read his notes.

His profession of catching criminals unawares had taught him to walk noiselessly. ('Like a prowling cat,' was Vince's verdict.) He had not lost that ability and suddenly discovered that he was not alone. From the other side of the stone benches, which were high and placed back to back, a small figure emerged with a startled exclamation.

A boy, aged about twelve he thought, with a book in hand. He had not heard Faro's approach and now, blushing scarlet, he bowed. The miniature frock coat, striped trousers, winged collar and college tie indicated a pupil.

'My apologies, sir. I – I am just leaving.'

Faro smiled. 'Not at all. I believe you were here first.'

The boy came fully into the light, still clutching his book and

Faro was amused to see, in large gold letters, *The Complete Works of William Shakespeare.*

Faro warmed to the young reader, for he had a similar edition at home, the last birthday gift from his beloved Lizzie. He never tired of the plays and sonnets and it was the companion of many of his travels. After so many years, travel-worn with loose pages here and there and generally dog-eared, its decrepit appearance managed to offend Imogen's sense of tidiness. She was constantly threatening to buy him an up-to-date edition and he was equally as constantly saying he didn't want one. This was an old friend, its companionship older than her own and that was that!

The boy, aware of his gaze, clutched the volume self-consciously. 'I have to learn Mark Antony's speech for tonight. We are to entertain a very important guest.'

Faro smiled. 'Indeed.' He decided it would be very unfair to add to the boy's embarrassment by saying, 'I am he.' Instead he asked, 'Do you like Shakespeare?'

'Oh, very much indeed, sir. I should like to be an actor.' A shake of the head. 'Although I don't care for learning speeches.'

'Neither do I,' was the sympathetic reply.

A good-looking boy with fair hair tending to curl, deep blue eyes, good features, tall and slim. Faro had seen someone who this boy reminded him of, something in his manner, but the devil of it was that he couldn't think where. He certainly had presence and looks enough to suggest he would make an actor.

'I have often thought I would like to run away and go on the stage. It would have been easy had I lived in Shakespeare's day, sir, boys played all the female roles. Though I should not care greatly for that,' he added hastily. 'I'd rather be Julius Caesar than Lady Macbeth.'

Faro laughed. 'Is there any reason why you should not be an actor when you leave college?'

The boy coloured slightly. 'My mother – she would never permit it – I have other ob- ob- obligations, you see.'

20

That sounded like a set piece. 'But I do like Shakespeare very much. He is my favourite since I came to Bri- to Glenatholl.'

'You are not English?'

'No, sir. I – I – ' He looked round suddenly confused. 'I must go. I am to play cricket now. I am in the house eleven.'

Faro smiled. 'It was good to meet you, young sir. Good luck with your speech – and your prospects.'

The boy bowed. 'Thank you, sir.' And with an endearing shy smile, 'I hope our famous speaker is as nice as you.' After that little speech and another bow, he leapt down the steps and was away, hurrying down the avenue between the Roman senators.

Faro watched him go, remembering that the school rules undoubtedly held a clause indicating that boys were forbidden to talk to strangers in the grounds and, further, that it was not good form, quite impolite really, ever to talk about themselves or refer to their elevated position in society.

The college prided itself (according to Vince) or pretended to firmly abide by the principle that, 'A man's a man for a' that' although Faro guessed they would have singularly failed to put Robert Burns at his ease or his maxim to the test.

The sun had disappeared below the horizon and Faro felt a shaft of chill and disappointment. Suddenly the grounds seemed empty and the gazebo cold without the schoolboy's welcome. A boy whom he would never meet again but who had shared with him, quite unknowingly, the bond of William Shakespeare.

The Bard does unite unlikely people from many different backgrounds and walks of life, Faro decided proudly, making his way – or so he believed – k through the midst of the senators now throwing long dark and denly forbidding shadows across his path as he valiantly tried to memorise 'Crime In Our Society'.

Now full of misgivings – why on earth had he chosen such a pompous title? he thought in despair – he tried to inject much needed humour into his opening remarks, mentioning the pupil who had made him welcome to Glenatholl.

Expecting to emerge on to the drive, he found himself in dense undergrowth. Where was the gate from the walled garden? Head down, thinking about that accursed speech – Dammit – somewhere he had taken the wrong turning.

Taking out his watch, he groaned aloud. Forty minutes and he would be standing on the platform in the dining-hall with over a hundred eager faces turned towards him, hanging on every word.

'Dammit,' he said again with not the least idea where he was. The grounds could cover a vast estate. Hadn't Vince told him there was also a golf course to prepare the pupils for Scotland's national heritage?

Was it too much to expect signposts? There were, quite naturally, none. Suddenly he panicked.

Then at last he heard horses, the rumble of a carriage near at hand. He must be near the drive. And so it was that the driver was startled out of his wits by a figure emerging from the rhododendron bushes frantically waving his arms.

'Can you direct me to the school?'

'I can, sir. I am going there myself. Jump in.'

'I am most grateful to you.' The man looked at him, observing the papers he was clutching. 'Inspector Faro, is it not?' When Faro bowed he said. 'Glad to meet you. You are tonight's speaker.'

The man introduced himself as one of the governors, but his name, amid the creaking of the carriage on the uneven drive, slipped by Faro who felt it would be impolite to ask him to repeat it.

'I am so looking forward to your talk. There are many questions about your career which have long intrigued me.'

Faro nodded, but hardly listened, acutely conscious that time was short. Then, at last, a distant prospect of the school arose. Richly turreted, it was yet one more imitation Balmoral Castle, not a style of architecture that Faro admired, preferring the classical Georgian style.

There were boys still on the cricket pitch and, walking down the middle of the drive, two uniformed pupils carrying bats. Faro had little difficulty in recognising the two men close at their heels as discreet bodyguards.

The two boys, one fair, one dark, their faces partially concealed by the deepening shadows, turned towards the carriage. At that instant the two men also stopped, hands shot out on to the boys' shoulders, instinctively protective. One of the pair, by the way his right hand moved fast in the direction of his greatcoat pocket, was obviously armed.

Such things were no doubt passed over unnoticed by the ordinary guests or visitors but many years of experience equipped Faro to observe matters irrelevant to the casual eye. And Vince had reminded him that the college was chosen for the education of many sons of royal houses. Doubtless they had bodyguards, thinly disguised as servants.

As the carriage flashed by, Faro had a glimpse of his companion from the gazebo, the boy he had so briefly met with Master Shakespeare tucked under his arm.

A rumble across a gravelled forecourt and the carriage had reached the steps of the college. There waiting to greet him was the Headmaster and a group of teachers in a flutter of black gowns.

'Such an honour to have you, sir. Especially on Founder's Day, the great occasion of the year for us.'

Introduced briefly to the group, shaking hands and with Headmaster Banes in the lead, Faro was brought into the vast panelled hall. Up the grand staircase with its stained glass window proudly sporting the Glenatholl coat of arms, his progress was marked by the gaze of portraits, benign, forbidding or merely superior, of former headmasters.

'We have put you in the Gladstone Room, sir. Mr Gladstone usually honours us with his presence on Founder's Day,' the Headmaster added in reverent tones: 'He gives a splendid talk, but alas, we were unable to have him this year. Quite unfortunate.'

And since they didn't get him, Faro realised, he had been second choice, though he was sure that had not been intentionally implied. Banes showed him into the room, and consulting his watch anxiously, hoped tactfully that half an hour would be adequate preparation.

'We will have the chance of a nightcap together with members of the staff in my study when the evening's activities are over,' he added soothingly. 'And a little extra entertainment provided by our very talented young pupils.' Faro had little difficulty in guessing that scenes from Shakespeare would be included as a special treat for their visitor.

Preparing to leave him, the Headmaster looked sternly around the room, letting his gaze rest on immaculate bedcovers, smoothly draped curtains and a bedside carafe of drinking water. 'I trust you will find everything necessary for your comfort, sir. We will send someone to tell you when we are ready for you.'

Faro was delighted to find that Mr Gladstone's room was equipped with the modern innovations of adjoining bathroom and water closet. There were towels and ewers of warm water. He shaved and at five minutes to five, earlier than he expected, there was a tap on the door.

He glanced in the mirror, picked up his notes and, taking a deep breath, opened the door. But instead of standing aside for him to leave, the man, a servant he presumed, darted into the room.

'I must speak to you, sir. I know you are Inspector Faro. I have heard about you. An important matter I must discuss with you – a matter of life or death,' he added dramatically.

His stilted English was to be expected in this college with so many pupils from far-off lands, and Faro sighed inwardly. He was becoming accustomed to this kind of thing, for having laid aside crime investigation, his reputation continued to follow him. Prepared to be patient and tolerant, since his retirement, he had often been accosted by someone who thought they had witnessed a crime or had certain knowledge of a crime that was about to happen. Or, most often, they required his help to track down a fraud case, a

misplaced last will by which they should have been sole bene-
ficiary.

He looked again at the man. Now bare-headed, was he one of the
bodyguards he had briefly glimpsed on the drive with the two
schoolboys? But as recognition dawned there was another tap on
the door.

'Enter,' Faro called.

It was one of the masters. He bowed. 'We are ready for you now,
sir. If you will accompany me – ' His frowning glance in the
direction of Faro's visitor clearly indicated that he wondered what
he had interrupted, and that the man had no business in this region
of the house.

Faro looked at the bodyguard, smiled and said, 'Come and speak
to me later. I must go now, I'm sorry – you can see – '

The man gave him a despairing look, a bow and departed.

As Faro seized his notes, he felt a shaft of fear. One of his strange
intuitions of danger.

Danger to himself? Perhaps – 'a matter of life or death'?

4

The Founder's Day talk went well despite Faro's misgivings. Questions were invited but they were few in number and from the masters who seemed to particularly relish the sound of their own voices. In one notable case, Faro felt he was in danger of listening to yet another lecture, on the moral obligations of a policeman, which was a novelty to the speaker and, judging by a restive audience, a bore to the pupils.

Faro's talk was applauded politely, the boys perhaps a little in awe of the great detective, although he had tried to be friendly and put them at ease by humanising his talk with amusing anecdotes against himself.

He noticed that the boy from the gazebo and his companion were seated in the second row. Behind them their bodyguards, one he recognised as the man who had come to his room just before the lecture to talk to him on a matter of great urgency.

The elder boy was dark, with high Tartar cheekbones, a complete contrast to the one he had already encountered who had almost classical good looks and who later that evening acquitted himself well in his Mark Antony speech.

There was no programme for the entertainment and the boy had been thanked by the Headmaster merely as 'George'. Presumably his identity was well-known to everyone but Faro. In the interests of the college's much-vaunted liberalism, all the performers were referred to by Christian names only.

George's companion was the star of the evening, a convincing Prince Arthur in King John pleading tearfully for his life. He received well-deserved applause.

'Well done, Anton,' said the Headmaster. 'Well done, boys.'

As the young actors returned to their seats, George continued to remind Faro of someone he knew. The devil of it was that he could not think who, or where they might have met before. However, since George was a common British name, Faro decided that the boy was most probably related to the swarm of minor European royals invited to Balmoral each year by the Queen. As most were of the same blood-line, there was often a striking resemblance to the house of Hanover.

Released at last from what had seemed like an interminable procession of scenes from Shakespeare, well-meant, well-played but an addition to the evening which he could have well done without, Faro was looking forward to the 'nightcap' in the Head-master's study.

Politely sipping a glass of sherry, his hopes immediately shat-tered for something stronger like a dram of good whisky, he chatted politely to the very important invited guests, the governors, masters and their wives.

It was soon obvious that his lecturing was not quite at an end as he was called upon by various individuals to answer a number of rather naive questions about criminal activities. These mostly concerned the apprehension of jewel thieves, a pressing anxiety and obsession of the wealthy.

As he answered as best he could he realised how sheltered were their lives. How sadly unaware they were of the dreadful measure of city violence amongst those poor humans, that lost stream of society they would shudder away from as their inferiors.

Released at last, he retired to Gladstone's heavily panelled room and sent a picture postcard of the school, from the stationery in the writing desk, to Imogen.

Around him impressive became oppressive, since every available space on mantelpiece and wall was occupied by almost as many pictures of the Royal Family as he had in Sheridan Place. Signed and presented to him, unwillingly displayed and discreetly removed, his wishes for an uncluttered desk were ignored as all were reverentially restored by Mrs Brook, Olivia and even Vince, when his back was turned.

Yawning, he lit a pipe and decided it had been a somewhat longer day than he was used to. But having promised to talk to the bodyguard who had appeared earlier that evening and at such an inappropriate moment, he felt obliged to wait a while before preparing for bed.

Certain that he would never sleep in that monumental bed, he nevertheless drifted away in the armchair by a dying fire to be awakened by the sound of rapid footsteps and raised voices in the corridor outside.

Was it a fire alarm? he wondered anxiously.

Opening the door, he looked out. A master, dressing-gowned and very flustered said, 'A slight disturbance, sir. One of the boys sleepwalking I expect. It does happen.' His smile was strained, even lamplight could not conceal his anxiety.

'Sorry you've been disturbed, sir. Nothing for you to worry about. Our apologies – these things do happen,' he repeated and with a quick bow he was off, speeding down the corridor and out of sight.

At last silence reigned. The clock on the college tower struck midnight. He had slept longer than he thought and as there was no possibility of his visitor arriving now, he prepared for bed. Perhaps the bodyguard had second thoughts, perhaps it was not so much a matter of life and death but an imperfect way of explaining something in English.

No doubt if the matter was serious, the man would seize some opportunity of communicating with him in the morning. Yawning again, he climbed into bed, and despite his misgivings, fell asleep.

He was awakened at dawn by pleasing country sounds, cows mooing, a cock crowing, horses trotting and a flock of quarrelsome sparrows airing their grievances on the roof above his head.

A maid appeared with a breakfast tray. He could not avoid seeing that she was upset. She looked scared and her hands trembled.

'Something wrong, my dear?' he asked, thinking as he did so that he was probably letting himself in for a tale of woe concerning a sad love affair, or a disagreement with matron.

But this was distress of a different kind.

'One of the servants, sir. He fell out of a dormitory window last night. He was trying to close it, leaned out too far. Slipped and fell – right down on to the flagstones. He's dead', she ended on a shrill note.

While sympathising with her distress, Faro considered the folly of boys' windows being open on what had been a very chilly night.

Doubtless, he thought, one of the spartan conditions of life in a public school. He realised that this unfortunate accident had been the disturbance, dismissed as a sleepwalking pupil, that was not supposed to trouble him. 'These things do happen.'

Faro wanted to know more. His blood was up, here was a mystery in the making, in the most unlikely setting of Glenatholl College. He was at it again, as Vince would say, aware that he must steel himself against a regrettable tendency even in retirement to treat every accident as a potential investigation.

Breakfasted, with still no sign of his urgent visitor of last night, who had perhaps thought better of that 'matter of life and death' after a good night's sleep, Faro was ready to leave the sanctuary dedicated to Prime Minister Gladstone. In the cold light of day he was now regretting the impulse to spend a few hours with his old friend at Arles Castle, consumed with anxiety for any official news regarding Amelie.

He picked up his valise and glanced briefly in the mirror. Startled by what he saw, he looked a second time. But before he could sort out some very weird thoughts, there was a tap on the door. Ah, the bodyguard – at last. He did choose inopportune moments.

Faro opened the door to a prefect who said that the Headmaster was waiting to bid him farewell. At the foot of the staircase, Banes asked if he had slept well and thanked him again for his magnificent and interesting lecture.

'Very unfortunate,' he said, in reply to Faro's question about the accident last night. 'A loose catch on the window. One of the, er, servants – a foreigner, alas – didn't know about such things.'

'Indeed. Who was this foreign gentleman?'

The Headmaster looked uncomfortable. 'No one you would know, Inspector. Pray do not concern yourself about our domestic affairs. They are trying, very trying indeed, and inconvenient. But such things happen.'

Again that phrase, now curiously doom-laden, and observing Faro's expression, the Headmaster added gently, 'I can see it in your face, sir. How readily the mind of a great detective turns to crime. But, let me assure you, if this was a case for concern then we have a very adequate and, if I may say so, very efficient police force.'

And that, Faro thought, put him nicely in his place.

However, as the Arles carriage arrived at the front door, it was closely followed by one Faro, from long acquaintance, recognised immediately as a police carriage, dark and discreet, with curtained windows. As a man emerged, there was nothing for it. The Headmaster had to make an introduction.

'Inspector Crane.'

The Inspector was a young man and Chief Inspector Faro's name had been a legend for a very long time. Such a long time, in fact, that as the Headmaster explained about the Founder's Day lecture, Crane was obviously taken aback to find Chief Inspector Faro was not only still active but still alive.

'Very pleased to meet you, sir,' he said in awed tones.

'An excellent lecture on crime in our society, Inspector. It would have interested you. Nothing to do with the unfortunate accident that brings you here,' the Headmaster added flippantly.

'Indeed no, sir. I'm sure such wicked deeds never occurred to your boys,' said Crane and Faro noted a touch, the merest flicker, of sarcasm in his tone. 'Anyway, we mustn't delay you, sir, this is a purely routine matter.'

Indeed, 'Did it happen often?' was Faro's unspoken question as he contemplated the prospect of more than a hundred normal specimens of boyhood, of mixed temperaments and nationalities, all bored with respectability and hell-bent on mischief.

'We must let you get on with your retirement, sir,' Crane added heartily. 'No need to worry. We're pretty smart here in Perth Police, we know what we're about.'

And Faro had to leave. In a mood of sudden exasperation, he acknowledged that there was no way he could follow Inspector Crane and sit in on the enquiry. It might have ended there had he not witnessed a scene as the carriage halted at a corner of the drive.

George was running ahead, with Anton trying to console him, for he was clearly upset. Behind them, panting in the rear, one of the bodyguards. Only one.

As the carriage swept past, Faro heard the bodyguard shout, and even with his inadequate German Faro knew what 'verboten' meant.

And where was the other bodyguard? The one who was in such distress but had failed to visit him after the lecture?

Suddenly he knew the answer. The foreign bodyguard who had wanted to talk to him so urgently was not an admirer of the reported exploits of Inspector Faro, not someone with a domestic problem, or there to request the autograph of a famous policeman. It *had* been, as the man said, a matter of life or – in his case – death.

And Faro knew he would never forgive himself for not delaying, and being five minutes late in taking his place before the college audience. What had happened in this instance to his much-vaunted intuition, his awareness of danger?

Tragic future events were to confirm his regrets.

If only he had listened, danger might have been averted, an assassin apprehended. His target a boy, a pupil at Glenatholl and a foreign royal, was in the deadliest of danger, his mother shot − perhaps fatally − and his kingdom in peril.

And Faro himself would not be spared.

5

Arles Castle was considerably older than Balmoral, somewhat worn and down-at-heel, its arrow-slitted exterior walls scarred by the bullets of Scotland's turbulent history. The turrets were no nineteenth-century architect's fairy-tale fantasy but had been built long ago with the practical purposes of defence in mind, including such niceties as pouring boiling oil on troublesome enemies.

Faro followed a footman to the upper apartments, pleasantly surprised that the occupants were untroubled by modernisation and the present craze for ornate ceilings and cornices. Instead the untreated stone was covered here and there by ancient tapestries and ragged old battle flags hung from the rafters. No handsome swirling oak staircase either, just a winding spiral stair, narrow for defence.

Sir Julian was waiting to make him warmly welcome with a hearty dram of excellent whisky pressed into his hand. As they talked, Faro considered his host. Approaching sixty, he retained the virile air of the distinguished diplomat.

An attractive, well-set-up fellow with handsome features, a head of thick white hair and a military moustache, the eligible and wealthy widower had disappointed many eager county ladies by marrying, three years ago, the pretty young woman who had nursed his first wife in her last illness. To his delight and the crowning glory of their domestic bliss, Molly had promptly presented him with a son and heir.

Julian's study was small, and warmly heated by a large fireplace. Beyond it was the Arles tartan-carpeted dining-room with massive refectory table, tall Jacobean chairs and tartan-covered footstools to elevate guests' feet above inhospitable icy draughts seeping under ancient ill-fitting oak doors.

After some polite interest in Faro's family – both daughters married, Rose in America and Emily in Orkney, Vince a flourishing Edinburgh doctor – Arles shook his head and said, 'Bad business about Luxoria.'

'Indeed,' said Faro, for this was the very topic he wished to discuss. 'Any news about the Grand Duchess?'

Julian paused to refresh the drams. 'There was never any mention of the extent of her injuries in the spray of bullets that killed the two servants. I gather the assassins had been lurking in wait for the shooting-party to return to the Kaiser's hunting-lodge. The ladies were riding in a carriage so it would seem that the Grand Duchess was their target.' He shrugged. 'Since there is no further bulletin, one can safely presume, I hope, that she has survived – so far. From my slight acquaintance with the lady, I fear she will be terribly distressed about those two servants who died.'

This was even better than Faro had hoped for. 'Your diplomatic career took in Luxoria?'

'Indeed it did. I was there fifteen years ago when the President was turning it into a military dictatorship, run by the generals under his command.'

'What was he like?'

Julian frowned. 'He was not a pleasant man. God knows how

Amelie put up with him. She has held Luxoria together for twenty years since her father died, a fearful responsibility for a girl hardly out of her teens. Even then it had long been a melting pot for potential disaster, situated as it is on three frontiers. President Gustav, like some latter-day Hannibal or Attila the Hun, seized power by a military coup and forced a political marriage on Amelie. She had no choice but to marry him. It was either that or exile.'

He sighed. 'Then the marriage proved, at first, to be childless. If Amelie hadn't produced an heir, Luxoria would have gone to the dogs and her death warrant would have certainly been signed.'

'Was she aware of that?' asked Faro.

'Indeed she was, very aware,' said Julian grimly.

A maid appeared at the door. 'Yes, Simms. Lunch in half an hour. That suit you, Faro? Where was I? Oh yes, Luxoria.'

And he went on to tell Faro what he already knew from Amelie herself.

'The situation between them was made worse – if that were possible – when it became widely known that the President had a son by his mistress. And President Gustav was so eager to replace Amelie, any excuse would do. Lord knows how she's survived so far in her own country, he must be quite desperate to get rid of her to risk an assassination attempt in Mosheim. What if the Kaiser had been in the carriage with her?'

He shuddered. 'An international incident that doesn't bear thinking about. The consequences could have been a war in Europe. Any excuse would do for countries who are watching Germany's policy of annexing smaller states.'

Julian regarded him thoughtfully. 'This is top secret, Faro – quite unofficial of course – but rumour has it that the Kaiser has indicated he would be more than happy to gather Luxoria under his own imperial umbrella, offer Amelie and her loyal countrymen his official protection. Certainly, Her Majesty would approve.' He laughed. 'Indeed yes, she would even add a grandmother's blessing.

I had that piece of information from Her Majesty's own lips. Very pro-German as you would guess and she loves to relate how her beloved Albert often theorised with the Kaiser's grandfather that he wished to see a liberated united Germany under the leadership of an enlightened Prussia.'

Julian sighed. 'I was glad to get out of Luxoria, and in one piece, I can tell you. Gustav's ambition was boundless. I fancy a case of "After Luxoria, the rest of Europe,"' he added wryly. 'A madman, but I imagine if Kaiser Wilhelm gets his way, he will sort him out. And despite his imperial ambitions, it will be no bad thing for Amelie. He's been her friend and supporter ever since they met, you know.'

Pausing, he smiled. 'It was at Balmoral in '78. I was an equerry then so I had a ringside seat, you might say. They were both favoured visitors, adored by Her Majesty and meeting for the first time. Despite the difference in their ages, or maybe because of it, there was an instant rapport between them. Amelie gentle, sympathetic and quite beautiful, was every man's ideal of a princess and I could see Willy, as everyone called him, was very taken with this lonely woman, unhappily married, with a young baby, who seemed to understand all his particular problems that no one else wanted to know about. And that did not include the physical infirmity of a withered arm, for God knows, the lad had gallantly overcome it through the years.

'He was nineteen years old and everyone at Balmoral knew he wanted to marry Princess Eliza Radizwill but, essentially Prussian in outlook, he had accepted the impossibility of alliance with a non-sovereign princely family. But he pined for his lost love. He carried her photograph with him. I understand he and Amelie wrote long letters to each other until their next meeting, six years ago, again at Balmoral, at one of those innumerable royal weddings.

'Willy had done his duty, made the best possible marriage for Prussia, but not the happiest for himself, with Princess Augusta Victoria, generally known as Dona, of the House of Augustenburg.

36

Once again the bond between two unhappy people was renewed. Once again both were seeking sanctuary and I'm fairly certain that was when Willy, an inveterate traveller, offered Amelie the refuge of his hunting-lodge.

'It's at Mosheim, near Heidelberg. Wooded country, on a hill-top, overlooking a river, picturesque and with stunning views. Twenty years ago while on a tour in the Odenwald, his parents discovered high above the town, in a forest noted for its wild boar, a picturesque but almost derelict medieval castle. Restored and modernised, they realised this would be the perfect setting for their shooting-parties.'

Julian shook his head. 'Amelie has been a regular guest, popular with even Kaiserin Dona, who doesn't regard the older woman as a potential rival although she's lost nothing of her charm for Willy. Poor Amelie, she's had such rotten luck. What's more, for many years she's gone in daily terror of her life.

'Her husband, she knows, has been behind several unsuccessful attempts to have her poisoned, and once the wheel of her carriage was tampered with and it went off the road down a ravine. The coachman died, but miraculously she and the young prince were thrown clear. That was just a couple of years ago.

'About this latest attempt, it must be obvious that Luxoria cannot survive the present turmoil in Europe and Amelie can no longer hold the reins single-handed. Seeing the results of the President's disastrous military rule I suspect she has needed little persuasion that the people of Luxoria would be better off under the canopy of Imperial Germany.'

For Faro, listening, many things were becoming clear and he was thankful indeed that he had accepted his old friend's invitation. Julian's connection with Balmoral was well known to him, but his link with Luxoria was an unexpected bonus.

'You think that was the reason behind the hunting-lodge in-cident?'

'Oh indeed yes. I can see President Gustav's hand very clearly directing the assassin's gun. Another thing, I suspect that it was on Willy's advice that Amelie decided to send the boy over here to school last year. An only child, she adored him, would do anything – ' he shrugged, 'even I suspect, turn Luxoria over to Germany in return for the Kaiser's protection. Doubtless it's a bargain package and he has promised to restore the boy to the throne when he reaches his majority.'

'A puppet government, you mean.'

'Exactly, but better for Luxoria than the ruthless man who has driven the country to the brink of anarchy and financial ruin by his excesses.'

'Surely Gustav has a good case for ruling in his son's minority?'

'You mean, God forbid, should the worst happen.' Julian shook his head, smiled wryly. 'If the lad is his own son, that is.'

Faro's heart beat louder than usual as he said, 'Indeed? The birth was heralded as the child of their reconciliation.'

Julian laughed out loud. 'I have always had my doubts about that. The premature baby, the oldest trick in the world. Remember the carriage accident Gustav arranged. He wasn't afraid that the child would die. In fact, that was probably his intention. Kill two royal birds with one stone – or a broken wheel.'

He shook his head firmly. 'No, I shouldn't be in the least surprised if Gustav knows or suspects the truth.'

'What truth?' Even to his own ears, Faro's questions sounded sharper than was necessary.

Sir Julian's eyes narrowed. 'Let me take you back to that first meeting between Willy and Amelie in '78. She brought the wee lad along with her, she was even then seeking a refuge from her husband. There was something I overheard – '

His eager look vanished. 'No matter, no matter. One must be discreet about such things.'

Faro was very eager to know what exactly he had overheard, but to his questioning glance Julian again gave that shake of the head. 'Whatever was the truth, I think Her Majesty knew what was what.

She and Amelie were often closeted together. Once or twice I saw them walking in the gardens, heads down, Amelie clearly distressed, bravely trying to conceal tears. I know enough about women to believe that confidences of a very personal and, I may add, highly dangerous nature were being poured into the royal ears, and that Amelie was over in Scotland precisely to take advice from her fond godmother.'

A thought flew unbidden into Faro's mind. Did Amelie come again to Scotland only to seek refuge in Balmoral with her son? Or was it a subterfuge, a yearning to meet him, let him see the child?

'Eliminate the mother first, then the son would be no problem,' Julian went on. 'If Amelie dies as a result of this murderous attack, then I wouldn't give much for the lad's chances of surviving to adulthood. Mark my words, he will be next,' he added grimly.

It was a terrible thought.

'You say he's at school over here?'

Julian grinned. 'Yes. Just a few miles from where you are sitting right now. He's at Glenatholl, no less. You might even have met him last night. Now, what's his name?' He frowned. 'John – no, George. Yes, George – a splendidly Hanoverian name for a Luxorian prince, don't you think?'

And Faro knew what had been tormenting him, why the boy had looked so familiar. He had unknowingly solved that particular mystery when he caught a fleeting glimpse of his own reflection in the mirror at Glenatholl that morning.

There were voices in the hall.

6

The arrival of Lady Arles, proudly bearing son and heir Augustus to meet Julian's old friend, could not have been timed for a less opportune moment. However, this interval of domesticity and the admiring of the new infant, who regarded him with deepest suspicion, was a blessing for Faro, a cover for his confused thoughts.

There were a thousand questions he wanted to ask, revelations that with a little gentle probing and a few more drams consumed by his host might bring forth a great deal more in the way of speculation than Julian was prepared to admit.

How infuriating – Lady Arles was to join them for luncheon. He groaned inwardly. Such a unique opportunity lost, a chance that might never come again.

Later he remembered little of the polite conversation that ensued, beyond Julian's nostalgic comments on days at Balmoral, accompanied by some excellent wine. Rather too much, in fact, Faro thought idly, watching one bottle empty and another appear. He realised he was allowing his glass to be refilled with alarming regularity.

By the time Lady Arles prepared to depart, having wisely refrained from the wine since she had an afternoon engagement (referred to by her husband as 'Another of your good works, my dear,') Faro had accepted their pressing invitation to extend his visit to include dinner, stay overnight and return to Edinburgh the following day. Behind this decision was the fervent hope of more confidences and revelations of royal indiscretions at Balmoral and elsewhere. But he knew this was not Inspector Jeremy Faro at his best. He desperately needed to think and think clearly, no easy task after the reckless depletion of the Arles' excellent wine cellar.

Most of all he wanted to talk about George, the boy in the gazebo at Glenatholl, whose face, a fleeting image, had been familiar. Dear God!

But confidences from Julian were to be further denied him. The estate factor, Lawson, looked in with some papers for signature and Julian, by now somewhat hectic in countenance, decided that fresh air would be a good thing. He wanted to show his guest the stables, the new horses, the old chapel. Faro trotted at his heels inventing ploys to lead his host back to agreeable reminiscences of Grand Duchess Amelie. But far off days in Luxoria were no longer on the agenda.

Julian excused himself. Estate trees to be felled and sold for timber. Lawson needed to show him the woods in question. So Faro went back to the castle and, in the room they had prepared for him, fell gratefully on to the bed and – thanks to the effects of the wine – slept soundly until the dinner gong alerted him.

Awakening in strange surroundings, his first thought was that it had all been a dreadful nightmare and he had dreamed that the boy he had met at Glenatholl was his son.

He sat up with a groan and a hangover of mammoth proportions told him it was no dream but reality. Worse was to come when he shaved in preparation for going downstairs and encountered in the mirror that fleeting likeness to the boy he had been in far-off

41

Orkney days. The face than now lived again in Glenatholl
College . . .

Sounds of merriment issuing from the drawing room dashed any
further hopes he had entertained of extracting information from
Julian. There were other guests for dinner that evening; nice,
pleasant country gentry with whom he had not one thing in
common and who asked the same questions put to him after his
Glenatholl lecture, about burglaries mostly and how they could be
prevented. And how thieves who were apprehended might be
discouraged from further wrongdoing by a hanging!

Faro was not a sympathetic or patient listener to the problems of
the wealthy for whom a few pieces of stolen silver that did not pivot
their world or throw it out of joint, were nevertheless regarded as a
catastrophe of fearful proportions. The conversation, or the wine,
or both, left him with a giddy feeling that instead of being within a
decade of a new century, time had moved backwards and deposited
the present company in the age of Hanging Judge Jeffries.

Faro made a valiant but useless effort to convince any of them
that much of Edinburgh's petty crime was brought about by the
necessity of survival. 'By men who would have qualities as honest
as any around this table,' he explained, regarding his companions'
shocked countenances, 'if they had work to do, and money to buy
bread for their starving families.'

Julian's applause and 'Well done, Jeremy' averted a dangerous
situation as did his call for more wine and change of subject to
the price of flour. As for problems with the tenants – 'Impossible to cope with them,' put in another guest, with a final
outraged glance in Faro's direction, 'Getting quite above themselves these days.'

Somehow Faro got through it all, retired most gratefully to his
waiting bed once more, slept well and, after an excellent breakfast,
was sped off for the late morning train.

Watching the carriage disappear down the drive, Julian realised that his wife's entrance yesterday had saved him from a major indiscretion. A scene he had witnessed in the gardens at Balmoral eleven years ago. A scene that he had discreetly kept to himself and, indeed, had tried to put out of his mind.

Walking alongside a tall yew hedge in the gardens, he had paused to light a pipe when he heard voices from a concealed arbour on the other side. Her Majesty and one he recognised as the Grand Duchess Amelie. She was crying. 'But he is so near at hand, could I not see him, just once? Just once, when the train stops in Edinburgh? I long for him to see his son.'

'Never. Never!' said Her Majesty. 'My dearest girl, you must never admit that even to yourself. You must put him from your mind instantly. To try to see him again, even to think of it, would be a disaster not only for yourself. Dear God, if you would be so indiscreet, at least think of the child's future.'

'But I do love him – still, to distraction,' was the agitated reply. 'I cannot bear it, that we are never to meet again.'

'Dearest girl, I sympathise. I know only too well what you are suffering. I have spent most of my life pining for my lost love, my dearest husband whom I will never see again on this earth. But you are young still and you must be practical and think of the scandal, I implore you. Think of what it could do.'

There was a slight pause followed by a warning. 'And if Gustav ever had an inkling, the faintest idea, that the child is not his, then you would have thrown away your kingdom. Please, my dear, dismiss this madness from your mind.'

Julian had crept away silently and he had never told a living soul. He was often haunted by the poignant scene and a mystery which had intrigued him over the years.

Indeed, he had been very tempted to tell Faro. He was the very man. The detective had lots of secret information concerning members of the royal family, for in his time Faro had had many dealings with Her Majesty. Yes, indeed, he could well be the man to know the identity of the father of Amelie's child.

It could not be Kaiser Wilhelm of course, Julian decided. But it might have been one of the royals Amelie had met during a visit to Edinburgh the year before George was born.

Whoever he was, good luck to him, for the outcome of that love affair had been a child who had saved Amelie's life and given a future to Luxoria.

Faro was still feeling very out of sorts as the Arles carriage trotted briskly through the mists of Perthshire, the dramatic autumn colours having faded with alarming suddenness into the more normal gloom of monotone Highland drizzle. He realised he was paying dearly for allowing himself to be so recklessly indulged by Sir Julian's lavish hospitality, which included, he decided wryly, as much wine as he suspected was consumed over an entire month by Vince and Olivia entertaining dinner guests at Sheridan Place.

Excellent vintage no doubt, but it had shot his powers of clear thought to blazes, completely dulled his wits. And he desperately needed to think.

Now that George's identity had been revealed, he remembered the scene in the drive with the two boys and one bodyguard. The missing bodyguard was in all probability George's, the man who came to his room and wished to tell him something before his speech that evening.

'A matter of life and death.'

He felt sickened with remorse. Doubtless the bodyguard wished to confide some vital matter concerning Luxoria. Luxoria had always meant Amelie, now it also stood for George.

He groaned out loud. Perhaps he could have saved the man's life too. An accident, falling out of a window indeed! It was too banal for serious consideration. Doubtless that was why Inspector Crane was on the scene so smartly.

Would he ever forgive himself for not appearing just five minutes late on the platform in the dining hall at Glenatholl?

Matters were serious enough without this new incident, he thought, remembering Julian's first-hand account of political unrest in Luxoria, which even before Amelie's visit to East Lothian had been fast deteriorating towards revolution. What those intervening years had been like for her he did not care to imagine, or the situation which had led, as Julian hinted, to her desperate consideration of abandoning centuries of independence and placing Luxoria under Germany's protection. As Julian had suggested, this was doubtless the reason for her attempted assassination at her husband's instigation.

In the light of his present knowledge, Faro longed for an excuse to arrive at Glenatholl, see the lad again, talk to him, even ask some questions. Was he aware that his mother might no longer be alive. How much had they told him of her 'accident'?

The picture of his tears, of being consoled on the drive by his companion and the other bodyguard shouting that it was forbidden would remain etched in Faro's mind forever. But sense reasserted itself over emotion, as it had done throughout his life. Whatever happened, the last person who must ever know the true facts regarding his birth was Prince George of Luxoria.

As the carriage approached the railway station through the streets of Perth, being unable to spot a newspaper vendor was a further frustration and anxiety. Faro wanted only to be back in Edinburgh as quickly as possible for a bulletin regarding Amelie's condition. Inactive and helpless, patiently awaiting developments had never been a strongpoint in his character or a virtue to number among his nobler characteristics.

7

The carriage set him down in the station forecourt in good time for the Edinburgh train. Walking briskly back and forth along the platform to ward off the chill east wind, he observed a stationary railway carriage on a siding, seemingly deserted and without any engine in sight. Faro had no difficulty in recognising it, despite the lack of any distinguishing marks, as the royal carriage which would be attached to a normal service train between Ballater and England. With no longer the least nostalgia for having often sat in that carriage during his service with Edinburgh City Police, he watched curiously as a figure descended and quickly disappeared, hidden by the other side of the platform.

Faro wondered idly which member of the royal family was on an incognito visit in the neighbourhood. The Edinburgh train steamed into the station and Faro was about to climb aboard when a figure rushed panting on to the platform, recognisable as the man he had seen leaving the stationary royal carriage.

The guard was waiting to wave his flag, and obligingly holding the door open for the latecomer, Faro's foot was on the step when he was taken aback to discover that instead of a grateful acceptance of his help, the man seized him round the waist and dragged him bodily back on to the platform.

'What on earth? What do you think you are doing? Release me at once!'

'Inspector Faro, is it not?' panted the man.

'It is indeed, if it's any of your business. Now kindly allow me to board the train.'

Out of the corner of his eye he saw the guard with the whistle at his lips, the flag in readiness. His mouth had dropped rather open and he looked like a man who felt he ought to intervene but didn't quite know the right words or gestures required. However, Faro's assailant, for such he seemed, nodded briefly in his direction and at the same time produced a card and thrust it before Faro.

Faro groaned. He had seen it before many times. It bore the royal signature. The code-word uttered at the same instant brought his immediate attention to Her Majesty the Queen's command.

'You do understand, sir. Bear with me, if you please. I will explain and you can catch another train. I assure you this is of the utmost importance.'

And still holding Faro's arm firmly, as if instant flight was intended, he nodded again to the guard who, thankful that his intervention was not required, blew his whistle. Faro watched helplessly as the train steamed out of the station without him, and with an exasperated gesture pulled his arm free of the man's grip.

'I am very sorry, sir. Captain Reece, at your service.' This, with a respectful bow. 'Now if you will be so good as to follow me, I will explain. My carriage is outside.'

So it wasn't to be the royal train to Ballater, after all. That was a relief, thought Faro. Following Reece out of the station, he demanded angrily, 'What in hell's name is all this about? Perhaps you are unaware that I am now retired. And that means I am no longer responsible for taking care of Her Majesty's affairs. There are other senior detectives and here in Perth I understand there is

47

an excellent police force, who are perfectly adequate to deal with such matters.'

Reece did not appear to be listening. Ushered into a waiting cab in the forecourt, Faro consulted his watch impatiently. 'Will this take long?' he demanded. 'The next train is in two hours' time and I should like to be on it. There are urgent matters in Edinburgh requiring my immediate attention.'

Reece stared out of the window, craning his neck, a gesture which suggested even to the uninitiated that he feared they were being followed.

'Captain Reece, I am addressing you. Have the goodness to give me your attention.'

With a sigh, Reece sat back. 'I will do my best to accommodate you, Inspector, but once I tell you what has happened, perhaps you will change your mind.'

The man's sombre manner was unmistakeable. The fact of the royal carriage and his sudden emergence suggested a crisis.

'Her Majesty – ' Faro began.

Reece shook his head. 'No. Her Majesty is in no danger.'

'May I ask where you are taking me?' Faro looked out of the window. The carriage had turned into a minor road. He noticed landmarks from the route he had travelled the day before.

'We are going to Glenatholl College, Inspector.'

'Glenatholl, for heaven's sake!'

'No!' was the solemn reply. 'For Her Majesty's sake.'

Such flippancy further angered Faro. 'Indeed. As I was there only yesterday, as you are no doubt aware, could I not have been informed of what was the trouble? It would have helped considerably with my arrangements.'

'Helped, sir.' Reece laughed shortly. 'You couldn't have helped yesterday. It hadn't happened yesterday.'

'What hadn't happened?'

'Since you left there has been a kidnapping. One of the pupils was kidnapped last night.'

The stationary railway carriage in the siding at Perth suddenly slotted into place. 'A royal pupil?'

'Yes indeed, sir. We were here in readiness to escort him to Balmoral when it happened.'

'And who, may I ask, is this lad?'

'The heir to the Grand Duchy of Luxoria. His life is in the greatest possible danger.'

Faro felt as if he had been struck in the chest by a sledgehammer. He could not breathe for a moment, as Reece continued, 'Perhaps you have not seen the newspapers? There has been an attempt on the life of the boy's mother who is Her Majesty's goddaughter.'

He shook his head. 'This is not the work of some political fanatic, the whole future of a kingdom is at stake and secret plans were ready to have him returned immediately to Luxoria if – ' Reece sighed. 'If his mother should die. You get the picture, Inspector.'

Faro was speechless, shocked into silence.

'The Headmaster will tell you everything. When he mentioned that you were still in the area, a very fortunate coincidence, we knew we could rely on your help.'

Faro was no longer listening. Numbness was receding, his mind raced ahead, his suspicions confirmed regarding that accident with an open window.

'A matter of life and death.' Dear God, why hadn't he listened? The bodyguard's accident had been deliberate murder. Desperate to warn someone, he thought a detective would be the proper person. And his attempt to save Prince George had cost him his life.

Perhaps even now . . . No! kidnappers did not kill immediately. They demanded ransoms for their hostages.

But that thought did not console him. He could see a door opening before him, moving away from local crimes into the world of international politics where he was a stranger. There lives were cheap when kingdoms were the prize.

Faro shut his eyes against the terror of what lay ahead.

8

Despite Reece's sombre warning, Faro told himself again and again that if the kidnappers had wanted the boy dead they would have killed him in Glenatholl. A ransom, that was it. It had to be a ransom. But the thought did little to console him as the cab swept down the college drive and emerged through the rhododendrons in front of the house.

In the Headmaster's study anxious faces turned towards him, the other bodyguard and Anton, George's companion.

Could it be only yesterday that the boy reciting Mark Antony's tribute to Caesar had been informally introduced as George? No title, no identification.

That the Grand Duchess Amelie had chosen to send her son to Britain – no, to Scotland and only forty miles from Edinburgh – to be educated was an appalling coincidence. Doubtless she had her own reasons. Had these included the hope, a mere whisper, that fate would provide a chance meeting? Other than four words added to the newspaper announcement of George's birth, she had never communicated the dangerous secret that linked their lives.

Faro tried to suppress the turmoil of emotions that seized him. He must concentrate on the fact that there had been a royal kidnapping and obviously, his sinking heart told him, George was in mortal danger.

'If you please, Anton, tell Inspector Faro exactly what happened,' said Headmaster Banes. The boy looked scared and moved nearer to the bodyguard, addressed as Dieter, as if for support.

'George received a note that a friend wished to meet him at the walled garden, near the gazebo.'

The Headmaster sighed. 'These are forbidden areas unless the boys are escorted.'

'The gazebo near the statues of the Roman senators?' queried Faro.

All heads swivelled towards him. 'You know the area, Inspector?'

'Indeed, yes, Headmaster. I found myself there on my way through the grounds yesterday.'

The Headmaster looked disapproving and faintly suspicious. 'You were unable to procure a hiring cab at the railway station? We did offer,' he added reproachfully.

'I did take a cab but I decided to walk from the gates as I had time in hand,' said Faro, anxiety making him sound more irritable than usual. 'And I met the missing boy there. He was alone. Please continue,' he said to Anton, annoyed that he was suddenly the one being interrogated.

Anton shook his head. 'I told him he must not go, especially – especially since the accident to Tomas, his servant.'

'The unfortunate young man who fell out of the window?' asked Faro.

Anton nodded. 'George was fond of him. He was very loyal.' The pieces were fitting together perfectly for Faro even before Anton went on. 'I was against it but George thought this meeting might have something to do with what happened. He – he – '

Turning, he gazed at the Headmaster. 'He believed that Tomas might not have had an accident.'

51

'Explain, if you please,' demanded the Headmaster stiffly.

Anton took a deep breath. 'George believed that Tomas had – had been pushed out of the window.'

'Outrageous!' was the roar of disapproval. 'Of course it was an accident.' And to Faro, 'The boys read too many adventure stories, I'm afraid. We try to keep such drivel from them, but the books are smuggled in by the servants.'

Anton gave Faro a despairing look. He did not care to contradict the Headmaster.

As for Faro, events were rapidly building up to an ominous certainty in his mind that the bodyguard's death and George's kidnapping were connected. And in view of what he had been told of secret plans to annexe Luxoria to Imperial Germany, he had little doubt that these two sinister events in Perthshire's elite public school were linked with the attempt on Amelie's life at the Kaiser's hunting-lodge.

'He was very upset about Tomas and wanted to tell Mr Faro,' Anton interrupted his thoughts. 'A policeman might have helped.'

Faro stared at him, unable to say a word. He groaned inwardly at this information of another who had believed in him and he had failed, adding to his remorse for the man who had needed his help and had been rejected.

Worse was the terrible feeling that had he listened, he might have averted this potential disaster. Tomas must have been aware of a plot to kidnap George, and he had been murdered for that knowledge.

'Inspector, a word, if you please.'

The Headmaster drew him aside. 'I expect you have heard the grave news from Germany concerning the boy's mother, the Grand Duchess.'

'I have. But did the boy know?'

'Not from us. We were told to keep it from him, not to distress him without cause unless – unless the worst happened and then, of course, he would have had to be told and sent back home

52

immediately. This kidnapping puts a very different, a very serious complexion on the matter,' he added darkly. 'I'm afraid the information has leaked out and this is a deliberate attempt to prevent George returning to Luxoria. Be as discreet as you can with your enquiries, sir,' he said, leading the way back to the little group. 'Please continue, Anton. Tell the Inspector all you know. Everything, every detail no matter how unimportant it may seem to you.'

Anton nodded, and thought for a moment. 'The note suggesting a meeting was on his mother's personal stationery. He misses her very much.'

Another pang smote Faro as Anton went on. 'I wanted to go with George. I pleaded and promised not to tell Dieter,' he nodded to the bodyguard, 'but George would not listen. So I decided I'd follow and see what was going on.'

'That was very foolish, but very brave of you, Anton,' said the Headmaster proudly.

Anton shrugged. 'Thank you, sir. At first I thought nothing was going to happen. Then a rough-looking man, like a gypsy, came from behind one of the statues.'

'Gypsies, eh?' the Headmaster nodded. 'There are a lot of them about the district.'

'This man came out and was talking to George. He obviously wanted George to go with him, but George was shaking his head. I couldn't tell what he was saying. Then another man came and they grabbed him and carried him away.'

'Carried him?' Faro put in quickly. 'Was there no carriage?'

'Not that I could see, sir.'

Faro thought rapidly. No carriage was very unusual, and considering the scale of the grounds, suggested that George might have been hidden locally. But before he could elaborate on the theory, the Headmaster's frown in his direction indicated that this was an unnecessary interruption.

'Surely George was putting up a struggle. Surely he would not give in readily to such treatment,' he said sharply as if regulations regarding behaviour *in extremis* were sternly laid down in the college curriculum.

Anton shook his head. 'I think they had tied his hands and feet. I could not be sure though, I wasn't close enough to see exactly what was happening.'

'Of course, of course. You are not in any way to be blamed for your actions, which were quite courageous in such horrifying circumstances,' was the smooth reply. 'Pray continue.'

'I did not know what to do, sir. I thought about following them and then I thought – I thought it would be better if I raced back and raised the alarm, told Dieter. He would know what to do.'

'Quite correct, Anton, you behaved admirably,' said the Headmaster. And to Faro, 'The police were informed immediately. They alerted Captain Reece here. He had arrived in Perth with the royal train to take George to Balmoral Castle, as a guest of Her Majesty.'

'I have already told Mr Faro,' said Reece impatiently. 'All was in readiness. He had been invited to spend a weekend shooting on the moors before the family disperse and return to London.'

'What are the police doing?' Faro demanded.

'They are searching for the gypsies, according to Anton's description,' said the Headmaster, 'since he was the only witness of the kidnapping.'

'I would suggest they start their search nearer home. In the grounds, for instance.'

'Indeed? And what brings you to that conclusion, Inspector?' demanded the Headmaster.

'Anton did not see a carriage. Presumably the kidnappers could not risk a strange carriage being brought into the grounds, possibly stopped and questioned.'

Banes nodded and put in quickly. 'Correct, Inspector. That is our rule. The lodge-keeper at the gate deals with such matters. With our reputation for having foreign royalty as pupils, we get our share of the curious, you know,' he added, not unpleased at such notoriety.

54

'And since the drive is a mile long, Headmaster,' said Faro, 'it seems unlikely that a struggling boy, bound hand and foot, would not have caught the attention of someone, the lodge-keeper or a gardener. They could hardly risk that. So I would earnestly suggest that a thorough search is made of the estate and any outhouses. Presumably they will be awaiting the right moment for transporting him elsewhere.'

There were noises outside, the door opened and George, dishevelled and scared-looking, rushed in.

Faro had to restrain himself from rushing over and seizing the boy in his arms. Afterwards he realised he had lived through what were some of the worst moments of his life, wondering if the boy was in danger, or even dead.

At George's heels was Inspector Crane, looking very self-satisfied indeed. Faro extended his silent thanks and gratitude to him.

George looked around bewildered, as if he could not believe he was safe again. Squaring his thin shoulders, he assured the Headmaster that he was none the worse for his experience and was escorted from the study to be delivered into Matron's care by one of the masters. Begging the Headmaster's permission to leave, Anton trotted after them, obviously eager and anxious to be with his friend.

With no opportunity to question or even speak to George, Faro took Crane aside and asked what had happened.

'We found the lad, tied up and blindfolded.'

'Where?'

'He wasn't far away.'

'He was in the school grounds?' said Faro.

Crane frowned. 'Yes. But how did you know that?'

'An inspired guess, since there was no carriage involved.'

Inspector Crane nodded. 'Very astute of you, sir. Very astute. We actually found him in the old stable block which was part of Glenatholl House before it was extended into the college.'

'At least he's safe. Were there any clues to the identity of his captors?'

'Not one. However, our investigations continue.' Crane shook his head. 'The gypsy encampment has gone. Packed up, nowhere in the vicinity. We shall of course track them down.'

'You still believe it was gypsies?' said Faro who had never put much store by that particular theory.

'We only know what the young fellow, Anton, told us.' He sounded unconvinced. 'Actually we have no records of suspicious persons about the area. The gypsies might steal a few clothes from drying lines, but they are mostly poor ignorant craiters, few can read and write well enough to be able to concern themselves with international politics.'

'Have you taken the accident to the prince's bodyguard into your calculations, sir?' Faro interrupted.

'Of course. But there is no evidence to suggest foul play. An unfortunate coincidence.'

Faro was no believer in coincidences. 'Earlier that evening, he wished to talk to me. I now believe he had some vital information.'

Crane stiffened. 'Had he indeed? The proper authority for such information is the Perth Constabulary, Inspector.' Without waiting for a reply, as the Headmaster approached, he said quickly 'A bit of a storm in a teacup. Boys will be boys, sir. All's well that ends well. I'll leave it with you, Headmaster. Naturally we'll continue our enquiries and if we find any significant evidence we will let you know.'

And that cliché didn't quite fit the occasion either, as far as Faro was concerned. If the attempt was genuine for all its confusing details, then all was far from well and far from ending. He had an unhappy intuition that it was just about to begin.

9

Faro followed Inspector Crane to the door. 'I should like to see this place where the boy was found, if you will direct me to it.'

Crane gave him a sharp glance. 'You would be wasting your time, Inspector.'

Faro bowed. 'Allow me to be the judge of that.'

Crane sighed. 'It has all been taken care of,' he protested. 'Believe me, there is nothing to see. Just an ordinary old disused stable. You have my word that my men are searching every inch of it for any evidence. So far there is nothing.'

Faro was not to be put off. He was determined to carry out his own investigation.

Watching Crane departing, somewhat grumpily, Faro observed Reece hurrying across the gravelled forecourt, his manner urgent.

'Exactly the man I want to see,' he said. 'I have received a message from Balmoral. Her Majesty has decided that you are to take charge of the boy, see him safe to Luxoria. The royal train will take you to Dover.'

Faro began to protest but Reece swept aside his interruption.

'There is concern that the death of the prince's bodyguard, Tomas, who was attached to our own secret service, might not have been an accident. He was very loyal to Luxoria.

'Her Majesty said there is no man she would rather trust. "I have put my own life in his hands many times." Her very words, sir,' he added reverently.

'I keep remembering that occasion at Glen Muick. They still talk of how you saved her from assassination.'

That time was long past and belonged to a younger, more enthusiastic Inspector Faro, who had not yet tasted the sweets of retirement. And flattery would get Reece nowhere, he decided.

'It isn't difficult, sir,' Reece pleaded. 'There are quite excellent trains, the Orient Express goes through Germany,' he added eagerly. 'You can pick it up in Paris at Gare de l'Est and get off at Stuttgart as the nearest stop to the Luxorian border. They will send a train to meet you.'

He made it sound like a picnic day at Musselburgh, thought Faro, seeing all his easy life of sitting in the garden at Sheridan Place and teaching Jamie to play chess evaporate like mist on a Highland hill above Balmoral.

Regarding his doubtful expression, Reece continued. 'There will be a substantial reward, recognition for royal services from Her Majesty personally,' he added with a significant pause.

Was he hinting at a knighthood? It was an offer which Faro had already declined, much to his stepson's chagrin, as the last thing he had ever wanted or desired.

'As you know, Luxoria is very close to Her Majesty's heart. Anything remotely connected with her late husband, the Prince Consort, is deified. And the Grand Duchess was very closely related to both of them.'

Faro had heard all this before and he wasn't listening. He had been commanded and he could not refuse a royal command without some legitimate excuse, like ill-health or sudden infirmity.

He sighed deeply, he might as well do his best to please Her Majesty, once again. For the last time.

And quite suddenly, as Reece rattled on nervous and eager at his side, Faro's mind began to present a consoling sequence of not unpleasing pictures. Once they reached Germany and he had seen George and Anton safely delivered to the Luxorian border, then he could travel on to Heidelberg. And Imogen. Not a bad thing at all. In fact, the more he listened to Reece, the more it appealed as he realised this was the chance of a lifetime, never to be repeated. The first and last chance he would ever have of spending time with his – with George – of taking a lifetime of getting to know the lad in a few precious days.

And that, come what may, was the deciding factor. He was ready to take on any odds for this unexpected hand destiny had offered him.

He had never expected to see Grand Duchess Amelie again. Now he would return her son to her. If she lived, please God. If she did not, then George was heir to Luxoria.

A wave of paternal pride swept over him. A secret that could never be divulged, but how he would relish hugging it to his heart for the rest of his life.

And so it was all arranged by Reece with military precision.

On the following morning, once George had had time to rest and recover from his ordeal, the royal carriage at Perth Railway station would be linked with the express from Aberdeen which would convey both boys and Dieter to Edinburgh. There Faro would join the train at midday.

The travellers would include Helga, a servant at the school suggested by Dieter himself. She had left Germany some years earlier and was anxious to return to her now widowed mother.

'It is an admirable arrangement, necessary to have a maid's services. Helga will attend to the laundry and take care of the personal ablutions of the two boys,' the Headmaster told Faro.

Before leaving Glenatholl to catch the Edinburgh train, Faro insisted on inspecting the old stables where George had been found.

He invited Dieter to accompany him and the bodyguard stood around looking bored and rather cross as Faro examined the faintly discernible footprints, for the weather at the time of George's kidnapping had been dry. That was unfortunate. But Faro realised from the evidence that Anton's description of George's captors had been correct. One was a large man wearing heavy boots, the other smaller. The lack of a carriage and the use of the old stables seemed to confirm that Crane's suspicion of a practical joke by the boys was correct.

He wished he could believe it.

In Sheridan Place, hastily repacking his valise to include a passport and his revolver, which he prayed he would never have to use, while bravely fending off Mrs Brook's anxieties about how many shirts and sets of underclothes and socks he might need, Faro told Vince and Olivia that something very important had happened.

'I am going to Germany immediately.'

Olivia's immediate reaction was delight at this news. Her face brightened and her expression said more clearly than any words that she believed Faro and Imogen were planning to marry at last. He could only guess at her disappointment as he told Vince of his plans to escort the heir to Luxoria back across Germany. In the interests of sparing Vince and Olivia unnecessary – he hoped – anxiety, he made no mention of the events at Glenatholl which had brought this about, beyond saying that it was Her Majesty's wish.

Olivia looked pleased and proud at that, but Vince, whose chief concern was always his stepfather's welfare, protested.

'Do they know whether the Grand Duchess is still alive? The newspapers have been remarkably silent about the extent of her injuries.'

On his arrival in Edinburgh Faro had visited the special and highly secret department of the City Police whose business was the acquiring of such information.

'They knew nothing. No news was good news, or so they told me,' he said consolingly.

'Are you sure you want to be involved in all this, Stepfather?' asked Vince, unable to keep the anxiety out of his voice.

'I have very little option, lad.' Faro shook his head. 'Even I cannot ignore a royal command.'

'But she knows you are retired,' Vince protested.

'Yes, indeed. How very unthoughtful,' said Olivia. 'A great strain on you.'

'Wait a bit!' Faro protested. 'I'm not exactly decrepit.'

'Olivia is anxious, as I am,' Vince put in sternly. 'Besides, how do you deal with anything when you don't even know the language?'

Faro shrugged. 'I will cross that particular bridge when I come to it, if ever.'

Vince sighed. 'I do wish I was going with you, Stepfather.'

'Since you don't know the language either, we would both be in trouble,' said Faro. While appreciating their concern, his patience was running thin.

'I would very much like to meet this prince,' was Olivia's tactful rejoinder.

'And so you shall, my dear, when you see me off tomorrow,' said Faro, glad of her diversion.

They drove him to the station the next morning, where a very wide-eyed Olivia was ushered into the handsome royal carriage which looked so dark and unassuming from its exterior.

She curtsied to the boy, who took her hand and bowed. Anton did likewise, as did Dieter, while Helga curtsied nicely.

Olivia was charmed by George and so was Vince, in spite of himself and his fears. Already he had his suspicions that he had not been told the whole truth and that his stepfather was embarking on no ordinary assignment. Reading between the lines, a matter he had become skilled at in their early days, Vince guessed shrewdly that if some person or persons did not wish the heir of Luxoria to set foot in his native land again, then Faro's mission was perilous indeed.

As they watched the train steam out of the station, Olivia said, 'What a charming boy. I have never met a prince before and George is such a very English name.'

'But it owes its royal origins to the Hanoverians,' said Vince leading the way back to their carriage.

Olivia emerged from her cloud of euphoria. 'He doesn't look in the least foreign, not like the boy Anton. George looks more like, well, a Viking.'

'Precisely,' said Vince drily, for the resemblance to Faro was unmistakable and he hoped no one in Luxoria was aware of the outcome of the Grand Duchess's visit thirteen years ago. How after many barren years the birth of a premature princeling had followed her reconciliation with her husband.

Olivia looked at him wide-eyed. 'You think – oh, surely not – ' And with a gasp of astonishment, 'You mean – '

'Exactly,' said Vince, opening the carriage door. For once he preferred to be a man of very few words. 'And we would be well-advised to keep such thoughts to ourselves, my dear.'

10

The royal carriage allocated to the travellers was comfortable but not luxurious. With the Queen's spartan attitute towards waste and extravagance clearly evident, it resembled a small parlour and only the rigidly anchored seats and table indicated that this was a fast-moving vehicle subject to the vagaries of speed on a railway line. As their journey did not include overnight travel, a bedroom was not at their disposal. The carriage, although part of the train, was private and inaccessible to other passengers boarding at the stations they passed through.

Berwick, Newcastle, Durham, York and so to London where they would be shunted on to a siding to await another train which would deliver them to Dover. There the Wagons-Lits' specially commissioned ferry for the Orient Express would carry the passengers across the English Channel to Calais and then the luxurious and famed Club Train would take them direct to Paris and the Gare de l'Est, where the next stage of their journey began.

It sounded simple enough, a smooth-running plan efficiently activated by royal commands issuing from Balmoral courtesy of the telegraph service. Faro hoped it worked, content meanwhile with the opportunity to acquaint himself with his travelling companions, in particular young George.

He was not by nature a nervous man, in fact he carried a lifetime's guarantee in the records of the Edinburgh City Police of being reliably robust in the face of adversity. However, in this instance he exercised extreme caution over the efficiency of arrangements in which he had not been personally involved. Any unscheduled halt of the train and his hand flew by habit and instinct to his pocket for the reassuring presence of the revolver concealed there.

Once, just beyond York, a great hustle ensued, with men rushing alongside the train, shouting at one another up and down the line. Dieter also carried a weapon and Faro noted his reaction was identical. Both men exchanged glances, with one thought in mind as they looked quickly round for a safe hiding place for the two boys should the worst happen.

There seemed nothing worthy of comment but George had interpreted what might be happening outside. He had also ob-served the two men's gestures towards their concealed weapons and said in a matter of fact way, 'If there is trouble, I think it would be best if Anton and I lay down on the floor, out of sight.'

'I don't think it will come to that,' said Faro looking at him admiringly. A cool head, twelve years old and no signs of fear. Well done, George.

He looked round the little group, brave indeed. He had expected that the woman Helga might have trembled just a little, but she showed no signs of emotion. All was calm. Nerves of steel.

Afterwards he was to remember the significance of that incident and how George was the only one who anticipated danger.

A guard appeared at the window on the line below them and explained the sudden halt. 'We're off again. Just a cow wandering along the line.'

Anton gave a sigh of relief and sat back in his seat. Perhaps he had been scared after all, as he said to George in German (which Faro only partly understood, but got the gist of) that it was as well that the Inspector and Dieter were armed, for one never knew.

Until the wandering cow incident Faro had not seriously considered that any attempts would be made to stop George from leaving the country. Now he realised he had responsibility for George and the enigmatic Anton who, he gathered from Dieter, was a remote cousin who had been chosen to accompany George to Glenatholl. 'In case he was lonely and needed a boy of his own age, speaking his own language and from his own background,' Dieter explained.

Admirable sentiments, thought Faro, and a splendid opportunity for a paid companion. In the circumstances it seemed inevitable that Anton should also be returned to his own country, although Faro decided he could have been forgiven for wishing to remain in Scotland and continue the expensive education that being companion to the heir of Luxoria had given him.

Anton gave little away. There was a watchful, guarded air about the lad which discouraged Faro's attempts at conversation. Was he homesick and anxious, or devoted to George? Both, or neither? Whatever Anton's reasons, there was a distance, perhaps an instinctive resentment as his sullen glance often rested on his cousin. With little difference in their ages, it was understandable that Anton should be envious of the younger boy's privileged position.

Regarding Dieter, Faro could only speculate. He did not like the man or enjoy the prospect of his company all the way to Germany. He felt no rapport, no common ground and knew only that he had met many such bodyguards in his long career. He regarded them guardedly as shady individuals who gave nothing away, and Dieter fitted the pattern, his emotions locked behind an expressionless face.

Yet there was something, Faro suspected, something ruthless behind that cool mask. A mask for the man of instant action, and that should be a source of comfort for here was a man who would kill without hesitation.

Having presumed that the two bodyguards were comrades, once while the two boys were out of earshot in the corridor, he asked Dieter what would happen to Tomas. Would his body be returned to his family in Luxoria after the accident inquest?

Dieter looked at him in surprise, as if such an idea had never entered his head. Without any emotion, he shrugged. 'He will be buried in Perth.'

'Has he no family?' Faro asked.

'None. Arrangements have been made. We have no details of next of kin.'

Faro knew there were reasons for such omissions by men who led secret and highly dangerous lives. He looked at Dieter's cold face. 'Do you believe it was an accident?'

Dieter shrugged. 'Of course. What else?'

Faro ignored that. 'Even considering George's kidnapping? Did that not seem significant?'

'Not at all. What makes you think they were connected? A mere unfortunate coincidence.'

Faro had long since learned to distrust such coincidences. Would Dieter be of the same mind if he knew about Tomas's visit to Faro's room just a few hours before his death?

'A matter of life and death.' He was about to tell Dieter but suddenly he decided against it. He would keep that piece of information to himself.

'People have accidents and get themselves killed every day,' said Dieter, which was hardly consolation.

But killing seemed far from that little group as the countryside and towns flashed by and Dieter opened the connecting door to allow waiters to bring their meals from the restaurant car attached to the first-class carriages.

Helga, a large, solid woman of uncertain age, withdrawn and keeping her own counsel, was another enigma. Faro continued to be puzzled over Dieter's insistence that she should accompany them. She seemed content to stare out of the window, her fingers busy, knitting needles clicking over some garment in bright red wool. Had her presence been suggested by Dieter as a mere kindness, to allow her to return safely to her widowed mother? Such a thoughtful gesture did not quite fit Faro's summing-up of the man's personality. Had she been young and pretty, he might have considered there was a motive, even a relationship between them. But although he was watchful, they remained distant from each other, two people locked in some secret compartment of their own thoughts.

As for Helga's recommendation as a servant, Faro regarded this with the indifference of a lifetime spent fighting off danger with little time and a total disregard for personal comfort. Did it really matter whether the boys had clean shirts and underwear for such a short journey? Helga spoke only to Dieter. Faro did not exist, while the activities of George and Anton were studiously ignored.

Apart from the two boys chattering together, there was little conversation in the group. And that was in German, of which Faro recognised only occasional words. As Dieter and the boys always addressed him in excellent English it was then he made a sudden decision – that it might be a wise move, considerably to his advantage, to appear, as far as they were concerned, to be completely ignorant of the German language.

The hours slipped past, the boys played cards or read the books they had brought with them to the tune of Helga's clicking needles while Dieter spent much of his time in the corridor smoking very strong cigars.

Faro had brought *The Mystery of Edwin Drood* which had a special appeal to his own instincts for detection. Unfinished when Charles Dickens died in 1870, it lacked the author's brilliant drawing together of all those seemingly unimportant threads and minor characters in one of his famous endings. Now, as Faro read, he made special notes of any possible clues, deciding that a pleasant retirement task would be to complete Mr Dickens' unfinished task by inventing possible and logical endings of his own.

The last part of their journey was in complete darkness with only the lights of stations and of isolated cottages, under a canopy of bright stars. Tall trees flew backwards out of their path and, illuminated here and there by lighted windows, ghostly telegraph poles threw out metal arms that gleamed moonbright.

This mysterious landscape of the night gave way to the sprawl of the great city of London, a vast spread of eerily gaslit streets of tall houses, overhung by palls of smoke. Lines of houses with tiny squares of windows in their walls, bright as eyes staring out into the darkness, gave tantalising glimpses into rooms warm and welcoming in lamplight. Eagerly, Faro rolled down the window, and the thick smoke of a thousand chimneys drifted into the compartment, the smell of city life and human habitation.

Then London, too, had vanished into the night and at last, yawning and weary, they were in Dover, with the train settling by the pier where the Club Train's ferry was about to depart.

Tomorrow they would be in Paris. By evening the Orient Express would have set them down at Stuttgart. There another royal train would be waiting and Faro's role in the life of George, heir to Luxoria, would be over forever.

It was such a short time, he thought sadly.

11

Following the porter wheeling their luggage towards the Club Train, Faro was impressed by the new stratum of society in which he had been deposited. He was very conscious of his best tweed suit, tweed cap and boots, good enough for Balmoral Castle but very suburban when surrounded by men dressed in the elegance of fur-collared greatcoats and top hats. On their arms were ladies swathed in furs with *haute couture* outfits, and bonnets especially striking or outrageous which, he decided, he must try to remember in some detail for Olivia's benefit.

Even the air around the platform, as these passengers waved farewell to friends, was redolent of luxury and wealth, expensive cigars mingling with heady French perfumes.

As for Faro, he consoled himself on the grounds of anonymity, that their little group would not be worthy of a second glance in such company. If any had observed them with curiosity, it would be to dismiss their group as a family with two sons.

Perhaps Helga had her uses after all, he thought, and there had been method in including her in the party. Her unassuming attire consisted of a navy blue jacket and matching skirt, with an equally unassuming bonnet. Well-tailored but shabby, her garb had the look of being handed down by some rich employer, giving her the unmistakable brand of a poor female relation or governess, while Dieter's reefer jacket suit and bowler hat provided a nondescript disguise for his profession. Tutor, upper servant . . .

With the confidence of one who had dealt with such situations every day of his life, Dieter had elected himself leader.

'Leave everything to me, sir. I will make all the arrangements,' he said and gathering Faro's passport and papers he went off to confirm their booking.

Dieter returned and said: 'I have booked a single cabin. It is best that we remain together. In the interests of safety, you understand. A wise move, I think.'

Wise, but alarming in its implications.

And, at this reminder, looks were exchanged by the two boys, their laughter and excitement giving way to uneasy glances which Faro understood, even while deploring the necessity of that single cabin. If, indeed, they were being followed, it would be very easy to isolate the two boys and the group and staying together offered extra security, with Dieter and himself both armed and ready to deal with any emergency. But the thought of being closeted in a room of ten feet by eight with the constant smell of engine oil and the threat of seasickness remained distinctly unpleasant.

Faro looked at George. The boy was as much a stranger to him as the rest of the group and he wished he could have had more time to discover more about him. For once, Fate was on his side and the Channel ferry crossing provided that opportunity.

From the outset it promised to be a bad crossing with a heavy swell. Almost immediately after the ferry took to the open sea of the English Channel the faces of Dieter, Helga and Anton took on a pale shade of green. Faro advised them to retire immediately to the cabin and 'get their heads down'. They could hardly argue but Dieter, with a handkerchief stuffed to his mouth, looked anxiously at George.

70

'You should come with us, Highness.'

'No,' said George bracing his thin shoulders. 'I am perfectly well. And I want to stay on deck. I love storms. I don't want to miss the chance of experiencing a rough sea.' Exhilarated by the wind and the sharp movement of the ship, he laughed delightedly at the consternation on the others' faces.

'Are you sure you do not feel just a little unwell?' asked Helga, at last showing signs of concern for their charges.

'I feel wonderful,' said George, throwing his arms wide to take in the sky as the ship gave a particularly vicious lurch. 'Please go below and take care of yourselves. Mr Faro will look after me.'

The three needed no further bidding and lurched towards the companionway in great haste, leaving Faro and George to face the elements alone – and whatever dangers were threatened by the unseen enemies Dieter had predicted were following the heir to Luxoria.

'May I stay out on deck, sir?' George asked.

'Of course.'

'It is the best place, isn't it?'

'Yes, indeed. And here's a corner,' Faro pointed to a pile of ropes, 'where we can sit down and be sheltered from the strong winds. Are you used to these crossings?' he asked curiously.

'Just coming back and forward to school. In the long vacation, when I can see Mother,' the boy added sadly.

'Are you ever sick?' Faro asked.

'Never. Perhaps I have been lucky in the past.' And turning to Faro he asked, 'Why are you not ill like the other grown-ups?'

'I expect that is because the sea is in my blood. My ancestors were Vikings and I was born on an island. All my ancestors went to sea.'

'Where is this island, Mr Faro?'

'Orkney.'

George laughed. 'I have heard of Orkney.' And Faro's heart gave a sudden lurch when the boy added, 'My mother knew someone who came from there, long ago before I was born.'

And studying Faro again he continued, 'She will be so pleased to know I have met a gentleman from Orkney. A Viking too. Yes, you do look like one. Oh, I beg pardon, sir,' he added, completely mistaking the reason for Faro's confusion.

Faro laughed. 'Not at all. I am used to it. People think Orcadians are Scots, but we are actually from a different race. From the Norsemen, not the Picts.'

'Do you have your own kings and queens, then?'

'Not for a very long time, George. We govern ourselves.'

The boy nodded. 'I would like to go to your island some day,' he said wistfully. 'The idea appeals to me. We never see the sea in Luxoria, we are what you would call land-locked. We have only rivers.'

The sea was settling down, the wind had dropped and the sky above them swayed, a huge black velvet canopy studded with bright stars. From below deck drifted music, a small orchestra for the passengers' entertainment, the sound of laughter, of happy voices. Far away, faint lights bobbed on the horizon, glowworms in the darkness marking the shores of France.

George yawned. 'I am quite tired, sir, but I do not want to go below. I don't want to miss any of this chance of being at sea and I would rather stay and talk to you, if I may, sir,' he added shyly.

Looking at the boy's pale face, which showed more than his brave words the recent ordeals he had been through, Faro said, 'Indeed you may. You may rest your head here, against my shoulder, if you like.'

'Thank you, sir.' And the boy leaned against him gratefully.

Faro closed his eyes, content to have this precious hour, precious moments that some fathers enjoy for a lifetime.

After a while George stirred, yawned and said, 'Do you think I will ever go back to Glenatholl again? I expect Mother will want me to finish my education once she is well again.'

Listening, Faro wondered how long they would be able to keep the truth about Amelie's 'accident' from her son. Surely he would see a newspaper or overhear the dread word assassination.

'Do you like Glenatholl?'

'Very much. At least I did, now I think I am a little scared.'

He shivered. 'Mr Faro, why should anyone want to harm me? I have no enemies. I have never harmed anyone and I had – have lots of friends at school. None of the boys care a jot about – who I am – you know, about Luxoria and that sort of thing.'

And with a sigh he added apologetically, 'A fellow cannot help what he is born and princes and earls are not all that rare at Glenatholl, so why should I be in any danger?'

Faro realised he was thinking about the kidnapping.

'I was really scared. I expect I shall have nightmares.'

This was the chance Faro had been waiting for. 'Perhaps it would help if we talked about it. Would you like to tell me exactly what happened that day?'

George thought for a moment. 'Anton could tell you better than me. He saw it all. I never saw anything,' he added ruefully.

'How was that?' Faro was puzzled.

'It all happened so quickly. One moment I was waiting to meet this mysterious person who had a message from my mother – I know her personal stationery very well. She writes to me often, every week, you see.'

'Do you still have this message?' Faro put in eagerly.

George shook his head sadly. 'No, it disappeared. I must have lost it somewhere. Perhaps it fell out of my pocket while they were carrying me. I struggled quite a bit, you know,' he added bravely.

The note was more likely to have been stolen and destroyed than dropped during the struggle, Faro thought. And destroyed so that it could not be used in evidence. Especially as it was most likely to have been a clever forgery.

'I knew she was going on a visit to Cousin Willy's hunting-lodge

73

in Germany. He's the Kaiser, you know,' he added casually. 'Mother is your Queen's favourite godchild and the Kaiser is a favourite grandson. They have been best friends for a long time.'

Faro had heard all this from Sir Julian Arles and gently reminded the boy, 'You were telling me about the kidnapping.'

George frowned. 'I was waiting for this person who wanted to meet me and the next thing I knew, something – a cloak I suppose – was thrown over my head, and my arms were fastened behind me with a rope. They lifted me off my feet and a man threw me over his shoulder.'

He thought for a moment, as if puzzled by something.

'I'm sure it was a man. At first I thought it was one of the boys playing a game – a practical joke. I laughed and told them to put me down and pretended I knew who it was.'

'And did you?' Faro asked eagerly. This was a new piece of evidence.

'No.' Turning in the dark, George looked at him. 'I knew it was in deadly earnest when I struggled and fought but it was no use.'

'You said "they"?'

'There was someone with him, running alongside.' George clenched his fists. 'Mr Faro, I was very scared. This was the first time in my life anything dangerous or even unpleasant had ever happened. When I realised it wasn't a game – '

Faro interrupted again. 'A game seems an odd sort of thing.'

George smiled. 'Oh, the boys get up to all sorts of pranks. They love playing tricks on each other. But not this time.' He shook his head. 'I really thought they meant to kill me.'

'What happened next, as much as you can remember, exactly?'

'Oh, I shall never forget. Never. Although each minute seemed like an hour because I was so frightened, I knew I hadn't been carried very far. I heard a door open, I was in a building and they threw me on to the ground. There was straw – I could smell it. I knew it wasn't a game now and I was very frightened and I kept asking, "Who are you? Let me go. Please let me go. If it is money you want, my mother will pay you – anything – anything you ask for." But no one took any notice.'

'I heard the door bang.' Faro felt him shudder. 'I – I tried not to cry, Mr Faro, really I did, remembering the boys and how they would jeer.'

Faro wondered if any would, had they experienced such real-life terror, as George went on.

'But I was very cold and hungry. Then suddenly I knew I must not waste time being sorry for myself. That wouldn't help. I had to be practical and use my energy thinking of ways to escape. It was very difficult with my hands and feet firmly tied, lying there helpless like a trussed chicken.'

He thought for a moment. 'The worst thing of all was their silence. That they had never spoken to me, never answered my questions or told me why I had been kidnapped or what they were going to do with me. That was worse than anything, not knowing. That and the silence.'

'You never heard them speak?' Faro asked curiously.

'No. Not once. Not a word. Not even whispers among themselves.'

Remembering Anton's description of seeing the kidnapper talking to George, Faro found this extremely interesting, for it suggested that Anton had been mistaken about what happened.

George's account was more likely. The obvious and sinister reason for not talking to him was that the kidnappers where known to him, people whose voices he would recognise. And that, in fact, was the very reason he had first suspected that they were boys from his class playing another of their practical jokes.

'Anton said there were two men.'

George nodded. 'That is so. The older man carried me but there was someone else running alongside.'

'How do you know that?'

George frowned, thinking. 'The man had strong arms, a broad chest. Tall. The other one was smaller.' He shrugged. 'Perhaps even a woman.'

'A woman?'

'Yes. Although they didn't speak to me or to each other, I heard their footsteps. The man who carried me was heavier-footed than the one who ran alongside, lightly, quickly – like a woman or a smaller man.'

Faro marked down favourably that the boy had inherited the useful asset of observation, despite his terror. Meanwhile there were many more urgent questions the kidnapping attempt raised. Particularly George's reactions to his bodyguard Tomas's fatal accident at Glenatholl.

He was considering how to raise the subject tactfully without further distressing the boy when a door opened and Anton shot on to the deck, out of breath and distraught.

Terrified!

It needed only one glance at his face to tell them something dreadful had happened.

12

'I have been searching for you, everywhere,' Anton shouted. 'I thought you might – might be dead!'

'Dead!' George looked quickly at Faro. 'In English, Anton, so that Mr Faro can understand.'

Flustered and shaking, Anton repeated slowly to Faro what he had said to George. 'I thought he might be dead.'

George laughed. 'Not at all. Here I am having a fine time with Mr Faro. Have you recovered from the seasickness?'

'Recovered!' Anton screamed at him. 'Don't you understand? I almost died out there. I was attacked. Someone tried to – kill – me!'

It was George's turn to look alarmed. 'What do you mean? Who would want to kill you?' He laughed uneasily. 'Anton, you must be mistaken.'

Again Anton turned to Faro and said slowly in measured tones. 'Someone has just tried to push me overboard.'

At his companion's dramatic announcement, George gave a horrified gasp. 'Anton – no!'

'Yes. It was like this. I was feeling better, not so queasy and as

Dieter and Helga were still asleep, I decided to have some fresh air. It is horrible being in a tiny cabin with sick people. I thought I would come up on deck and look for you but I turned dizzy again and leaned against the rail. That was when someone grabbed me.'

'What was he like?' asked George. 'Did you see his face?'

Anton hesitated. 'No. But I think – ' he hesitated, 'yes, definitely, a big strong man.'

And Faro's mind flashed back to the description of George's kidnapper as Anton said, 'He crept up, took me by surprise.'

Again Faro thought of the scene in Glenatholl's gardens that George had just described.

'He had a stick, he raised it to strike,' Anton continued. 'But I was fortunate. At that moment the ship lurched, it threw him off balance and I ran away as fast as I could.' He paused. 'That is why I am so out of breath.'

Before Faro could ask for more details George, who was clearly very doubtful about this little drama, asked, 'Are you sure he meant to kill you, Anton?'

'Of course,' was the angry reply. 'How could I be mistaken about that?'

'It could have been the ship lurching at that moment that threw him off balance so that he bumped into you.'

The voice of reason, thought Faro, amazed at George's calm and quite logical interpretation.

'No,' Anton shook his head firmly. 'I am perfectly sure he meant to throw me overboard.'

'But why, Anton? Why should a complete stranger threaten you so violently?'

'That is easy. Because he thought I was you,' said Anton triumphantly. And at George's horrified exclamation, 'Yes, you, George! We are much the same height and in the darkness, with my back turned to him. You see, I am wearing a cap and your cape – here.'

As he held it out, George regarded it wide-eyed.

'I picked it up to come on deck. Helga was using mine as a blanket and I didn't want to disturb her, Dieter was also asleep, as I told you. Now, what do you think of that, George.'

Dazed, George shook his head.

'So it is true, Mr Faro,' said Anton sternly. 'Someone is trying to kill him. They have followed us and they are here on this ship.'

Faro inclined to George's interpretation, since the alternative was very sinister indeed. But if Anton was not dramatising an accident then the killer had bungled his opportunity. He had run out of time for a second attempt, as the ferry was arriving at Calais.

Just then an announcement was made that passengers were to remain on the ferry until morning due to the breakdown of the Club Train on its way from Paris. There were cries of dismay and alarm at this news, though passengers who had booked cabins gave a sigh of relief and were not at all sorry to retire and continue their journey the following morning.

Faro was glad of Dieter's foresight and as the two boys raced ahead down the companionway he seized the opportunity of telling the bodyguard about Anton's alarming experience.

Dieter shrugged. 'He has mentioned it,' he said in a voice devoid of all emotion.

'And what were your conclusions? Do you think it was, as he believed, meant for George?'

Again that shrug of the shoulders. Dieter spread his hands wide.

'Who knows? It might have been an accident, but we must remain vigilant at all times. Expect the unexpected, as they say in your country,' he added as they reached the cabin where Helga and the two boys were waiting.

Full of a solitary sleeper's apprehension and resigned to spending a crowded night in a small space with relative strangers – all but George, for he was no longer included in that category – Faro was pleased to find that the four bunks in the cabin were at least roomy and comfortable.

'Where is Helga to sleep?' he asked.

Dieter's shrug indicated indifference to this matter. 'I believe she has found accommodation among the other servants travelling with their employers.'

The two boys were obviously very tired but brightened up considerably at being given a complimentary meal in the elegant ferry restaurant.

At last they retired and Faro hoped sleep would be possible since not all the travellers were weary. Most were in high spirits, already exhibiting every intention of whiling away the hours until morning with wine, women and an abundance of song.

As for Faro, he was surprised to find that despite his misgivings about the crowded sleeping arrangements in the tiny cabin, he slept very well. No dreams, or nightmares. No predictions at all of what the future held. No more danger than if he had been on a journey to Germany to meet Imogen and spend Christmas in Heidelberg.

But Jeremy Faro's optimism was in vain. And it seemed that his guardian angel was having an off day or his normally reliable intuition was once more letting him down badly and had taken early retirement.

They were awakened at daybreak by a waiter bearing a light repast of coffee and croissants, with fruit juices for the two boys. This was offered with due apologies as the passengers would receive a proper *petit déjeuner* once they boarded the Club Train waiting at the rail terminus by the ferry.

Their luggage already transferred to the baggage car, the five travellers made their way across the quayside, with the smell of the sea still encompassing them and the shrill cries of seabirds, who were particularly attracted to ferries after the breakfast hour.

A porter ushered them into a six-seater compartment and soon they were under way, on the first stage of their journey across France where, unfortunately, the landscape was blotted out by heavy rain.

The boys and Dieter played cards, Helga frowned over her

knitting, counting some complicated pattern, and Faro returned to his unsolved mystery of Edwin Drood.

At last the Club Train steamed importantly into Gare de l'Est railway station and the passengers were set down alongside the sleek gleaming teak exterior of the Orient Express.

This was the moment the two boys had been waiting for.

'I love trains, Mr Faro,' said George, clapping his hands and jumping up and down. He and Anton had to be restrained from tearing along the platform by Dieter dashing after them, grabbing their arms and muttered a warning in German. Something about causing embarrassment among the passengers. Whatever it was, it had some effect on George who continued to regard Dieter with an odd, puzzled expression.

The spontaneous excitement and exuberance of two young boys faced with this wonder of the age, travel by train, was well understood by Faro. When he was young and trains were in their infancy, the thought of tearing through the countryside at fifty miles an hour was a daring prospect, not for the timid-minded.

Her Majesty, who now accepted trains as the most convenient means of travelling between London and Scotland, had originally refused to expose her royal person to such unnatural speeds, quite against what God had intended for those He had anointed to rule over ordinary mortals. At last prevailed upon to risk a short trial journey to Stroud and emboldened by escaping unscathed, in the summer of 1879 she ventured across the newly-built Tay Bridge. In December it collapsed, taking 75 passengers to their death in the river far below.

Faro realised that this new generation would have very different attitudes to experiments with travel, if the two boys were any indication. Wild with excitement at the sight of the huge train steaming gently on the platform, George ignored Dieter's restraining hand and turning to Faro he said apologetically, 'I do adore trains. This is the most exciting moment in my whole life,' he added solemnly.

And Faro prayed fervently that was so, that nothing more hazardous lay ahead than a smooth-running uneventful train journey across France and Germany to the Luxorian border.

He was well-pleased with their compartment: comfortable seats padded against the motion of the train, to be adapted into small beds for the further comfort of passengers travelling by night, mirrors on walls of marquetried wood panels, curtains on the windows, a small table let down from the door frame for refreshments and an adjoining screened washbasin and water closet, much to the delight of the two boys.

'This is more luxury than we have in Glenatholl,' George pointed out.

The guard checked their tickets, followed by a porter wishing to stow away their hand-luggage and somewhat surprised that the older gentleman in the party preferred to keep his valise at his side.

Soon the two boys were bouncing up and down on the seats while staring out of the window at the platform crowded with onlookers watching out for the famous, or saying farewells to friends. Once or twice Dieter tried in vain to entreat the boys to remain seated, not to be vulgar was how Faro's limited German translated his words. But even Dieter had not the heart to quell their enthusiasm. Indeed, looking at the man's slightly flushed countenance, devoid of its usual calm, Faro suspected that he too was suffering from Orient Express excitement.

Suddenly, as the train prepared to depart, he realised that Helga was missing.

13

Faro turned to Dieter. 'Helga – where is she? Surely we aren't leaving without her?'

Faro's last sight of her had been trailing behind them as if she did not wish to be associated with the two boys' exuberant behaviour. It also suggested that she might be keeping a lookout for the ladies' toilet facilities on the platform.

Now Dieter shook his head. 'Did you not know, Mr Faro? I thought Anton had told you.' He darted a sharp glance at the boy, who merely shrugged at this matter of no importance.

Dieter gave an exasperated sigh. 'Helga has not been feeling very well, the crossing upset her badly. She is not a good traveller and she decided that she might be going down with a fever.'

'A fever?' Faro exclaimed. He found that hard to believe, Helga had looked perfectly healthy to him.

'Indeed yes. And a fever on the Orient Express could be a great embarrassment to us all, especially to other important travellers,' said Dieter, nodding towards the two boys who no longer had interest in anything but the train steaming out of the station. 'Cholera, you know,' he whispered.

Indeed, Faro did know. Cholera epidemics were the scourge of Europe, the haunting fear of every traveller on a long journey into foreign lands. There was a clause Imogen and he were now accustomed to encountering in all railway timetables, in very small print so as not to cause undue alarm: 'These schedules are issued, cholera permitting. The company does not accept responsibility for any illness incurred by its travellers during transit.'

'Helga is in a constant state of anxiety about her health, even when she is quite well,' said Dieter. 'She suffers from her digestion.'

That, thought Faro, was one answer to her rather flustered manner on the platform.

'The journey has been difficult for her,' Dieter went on, 'so she decided it would be advisable to spend a few days with her grandmother, who lives here in Paris, to recover before continuing her journey to Germany.'

Faro wondered when the silent and withdrawn Helga had imparted all this personal information to Dieter. Listening to the man as he talked, watching him closely, Faro decided he could hardly argue, although Helga had seemed robust enough on the Club Train journey from Calais, recovered from her seasickness and content to sit in a corner with her knitting. A smooth tale, well-prepared, he thought, but was it the truth? Again his aversion to the man brought a cold feeling of distrust, a twitch of his old intuition again.

And the sinister fact remained, what had caused Helga to so abruptly change her mind?

Once more studying Dieter, he made a mental note that he must never relax vigilance, that this man who had appointed himself their leader was an unknown quantity, a ruthless man, one who would not think twice about killing an adversary or of getting rid of someone who was no longer of any use to him, their presence an inconvenience. Especially if he was being paid well to do so.

The train was now gathering speed. Faro was helpless to do anything. He could hardly raise an outcry about a missing passenger and insist on the train returning to the platform while he went in search of Helga.

He bit his lip, frustrated. True, he owed her nothing, her attitude toward him had been indifferent, even faintly hostile, but he could not shake off the fear that some misfortune other than a suspected fever had prevented her from joining the train and continuing the journey with them.

'I wish Helga had told us of her intentions,' he remarked to Dieter, in a tone of stern disapproval.

Dieter grinned at him, a cold mirthless parting of his thin lips. 'She informed Anton of her change of plan.'

Confiding in Anton also seemed rather unlikely, thought Faro.

'You must understand that her English is very poor,' Dieter explained. 'She would have found it difficult to explain to you why she was leaving us, and perhaps feared that you might have objections.'

'Why should I have objections?'

Dieter shrugged. 'You might wish for a maid to look after us. Most gentleman in your position would expect such services. For the laundry and so forth.'

'I hardly think we will need the laundry on this train,' Faro said coldly. 'I imagine all such matters are well in hand.'

'I am sure you are right, Mr Faro,' was the smooth reply. 'But look at it this way. Is it not to our advantage and more convenient, as you will surely see, to have four males sharing a compartment – for safety?' he added emphasising the word. 'A lady's presence would have been difficult. We would have had to engage a separate sleeping compartment for her.'

'I had presumed you would have thought of that,' said Faro. 'Surely the train provides places for lady's maids and nannies travelling with their employers.'

Dieter gave him an angry glance. He did not like being questioned. 'I would have found accommodation for Helga once the train had started,' he said shortly. But was that all? Had Dieter regretted his impulse to bring her along, overcome by some crafty measure of thrift that Faro knew nothing about?

The man was an enigma, he thought, as Dieter shrugged and looked out of the window, indicating that the matter was closed.

But was it? Faro continued to have pangs of conscience about Helga, wishing he had taken more notice of her and that he could believe Dieter's story had some elements of truth in it.

The boys announced that they were hungry and when Dieter responded by saying they should all go directly to the restaurant car, they raced ahead and George cannoned into a crusty old gent.

'You should teach your son better manners, sir,' the man said to Faro.

Faro pretended not to hear, the significance of the remark lost upon him as he gazed at the elegant restaurant car. The walls were padded in Spanish leather, the ceiling painted in Italian stucco and at tables set with linen and silver, *petit déjeuner* was being served. Studying the menu he was unaware of Dieter's puzzled gaze changing into sudden enlightenment.

There were wine glasses and George, tapping one with his finger, said solemnly, 'Real crystal, Mr Faro, like we have at home.'

Faro smiled, for crystal was one of Luxoria's famous exports. It would have seemed an extravagance considering the possibilities involved in a swaying train, the kind with wooden seats and no facilities, crowded with people and all too often with their animals too – trains that he and Imogen were used to in their travels across Europe – but here was a machine from the world of the future, gliding along the railway lines so smoothly. Imogen would be so envious when he told her about it. He thought wistfully that some day in the future, if they saved enough money, they might manage a very short journey on the Orient Express.

Having observed Faro's anxious reaction to the possible fate of crystal glasses, George said, 'This carriage, like our sleeping car, is on bogies, did you know that, Mr Faro?'

Faro shook his head. The only bogeys he knew anything about were of the supernatural variety beloved of Celtic myths.

'Bogies make travel much safer as they allow the wheels to swivel independently of the carriage and this gives a smoother ride round bends,' was the knowledgeable explanation.

Faro smiled. 'You know a lot about trains.'

George laughed and said proudly. 'I once met Monsieur Nagelmachers who created this Orient Express. He came to visit Luxoria when I was quite small – four years old. He is a Belgian and King Leopold, who loved travelling on his trains, and was a great friend, came with him. The King was cousin to your Prince Albert, and liked visiting my mother.'

King Leopold was another of that great sprawling royal family of Europe, all of them related, near and distant, to Her Majesty Queen Victoria.

'Monsieur Nagelmachers told me all about trains, and he gave me a tiny model which I always carry with me. I'll show it to you sometime.'

Faro looked across at Anton listening expressionless to this conversation with nothing to contribute. And he guessed that George's not-so-privileged companion probably had less happy experiences of travel, similar to his own.

As for Dieter, he was positively animated. With an air of excitement he leaned forward, stared fascinated at George, then at Faro and back again, a smile twisting his thin lips.

Returning to their compartments, those passengers who were journeying across Europe with hopes of enjoyable continental scenery were in for a disappointment. The weather had deteriorated since they left Paris. Rain streamed steadily down the windows, obliterating a landscape which, from very brief glimpses, Faro found flat and disappointing, used as he was to the more romantic undulating hills of Scotland. Vast tracts of land dotted with sentinel lines of poplar trees and rows of dry-looking sticks planted with mathematical precision stretched mile after dreary mile, sticks that in the proper season would blossom into vineyards, their harvest served as wines famous across Europe in every high-class hotel.

Finding it difficult to concentrate on the problems of Edwin Drood, Faro turned his attention to his fellow passengers.

Dieter leaned back in his seat with his eyes closed, apparently sleeping, since he had brought nothing, not even a newspaper, with which to while away the hours. Occasionally his eyes flickered open, he yawned and went into the corridor to smoke one of his strong-smelling cigars.

After an altercation when Anton was accused of cheating and George seized the playing cards and set them aside, the two boys sulkily resumed reading the books they had brought with them. Faro was pleased to see that although Anton was reading in German, George had a copy of *Treasure Island* by Robert Louis Stevenson.

George sometimes glanced across at him, frowning. There was a word in dialect he wasn't sure about. When Faro explained, George asked, 'Do you know Mr Stevenson?'

Faro shook his head. 'No. But my stepson was at the University in Edinburgh when he was studying law.'

'He lives in Edinburgh?'

'Not any longer. His health is very poor and he plans to live on an island in the South Seas.'

George smiled. 'Will it be as nice as Orkney, do you think?'

Faro laughed. 'I'm sure it will be much warmer.'

Anton, once again not included in the conversation, suddenly put his own book aside with an irritable gesture and, picking up the pack of cards, began to shuffle them.

'Another game?' he demanded in German.

'Very well, if you promise not to cheat this time,' was what Faro understood as the gist of George's reply. 'Will you play with us, Mr Faro?'

'No, thank you. I'll continue with my book.'

But somehow his efforts to solve Mr Dickens' fictional mystery had evaporated in the face of a much more present mystery.

What had happened to Helga? His thoughts kept returning to her. And because his life's work was a search for clues in apparently unconnected events, he took out paper and pencil and wrote down:

1. Attempt on the life of Amelie. Possible connection with:
2. The fatal accident at Glenatholl of George's bodyguard Tomas.
3. George's kidnapping and rescue.
4. Anton's attack and escape on the ferry. (Note: A big strong man was described on both occasions. At Glenatholl, indications were that he had a companion. A smaller man or a woman?)
5. Helga's disappearance. Where did she fit into this curious pattern of events? And, more important, why had she been brought along in the first place other than as a gesture of kindness? Was there a more sinister reason? Had she been disposed of permanently?'

He was too preoccupied to realise that Dieter had also found a vital clue to the secret of Faro's identity. It had taken Helga with her woman's intuition to hint what was now strikingly obvious and Dieter toyed happily with thoughts of President Gustav's reward for this particular piece of information.

14

Faro's thought pattern was destroyed by the entrance of a waiter announcing luncheon in the restaurant car. The perfect antidote to possible boredom, though passengers had breakfasted only two hours earlier. Obviously this constant serving of meals to while away the hours was one of the spectacular luxuries of the Orient Express, a boost to flagging spirits, regardless of the weather beyond the windows.

The two boys cheered. They were always hungry and had to be restrained from yet another headlong dash down the train.

At last they were seated and an imposing menu set before them, calculated to tempt even the most jaded appetite: *Foie gras* served with Vienna rolls, smoked salmon, steak *tortellina* and an extravagant range of vegetables.

Faro looked anxiously at George and Anton since this was somewhat different from the homely fare even important visitors at Glenatholl encountered. He was pleased to see that the two boys tucked in heartily, undeterred by such a sophisticated meal, and how their eyes brightened at the sight of a rich chocolate *Sacher Torte* served with thick cream.

The waiter was not at all put out when Faro looked askance at their demands for second helpings. He smiled and said, in very good English, 'It is a pleasure. So many of the young ones travelling with their parents refuse the fare we have on offer and make a great fuss at every meal. Nothing ever pleases them,' he concluded with a weary sigh.

'When do we arrive in Strasbourg?' Faro asked.

'In one hour.' The waiter looked at the rainstreaked windows. 'However, we may be running a little late as I understand they have had a fall of snow.'

'Surely it is early for that?' said Faro.

'These things happen, sir.'

As they returned to their compartment, the outlook was very bleak indeed, the grey landscape obliterated by heavy rain. The approach to the railway station on the outskirts of the town was through a huddle of poor dwellings, tiny hovels crushed together, Faro imagined, by a ruthless builder, interested only in profits and with scant regard for human comfort. The houses were so close to the railway track that every passing train must have rattled them to their flimsy foundations. From windows lacking glass and covered in dirty rags, white faces of children stared out wide-eyed at the magnificence of the Orient Express as it thundered past, a creation from a world beyond their wildest dreams.

Remembering the luncheon they had just enjoyed, several courses of huge and elaborate helpings, Faro thought of the plates removed from tables, many with their contents either half-eaten or untouched. They would have provided rich sustenance for those starving families bordering the railway sidings. He felt disgust at the extravagance, although these were familiar scenes he and Imogen frequently encountered in the slums of great cities, they never failed to stir in him feelings of guilt, the indignation of a social conscience at the unfairness of the distribution of the world's wealth.

'Strasbourg! Strasbourg!'

The Orient Express glided to a halt alongside the platform and Faro rolled down the window, determined to take this chance of a breath of air.

As the clouds of steam diminished he looked towards the departing passengers. There was one he recognised. A figure in a navy-blue jacket and skirt, with an unmistakeable shabby bonnet, hurrying towards the exit.

'Helga!' he shouted. 'Helga! Wait!'

The woman half-turned, glanced back briefly and disappeared in the crowd.

'Helga!' Faro shouted again.

Dieter looked over his shoulder. 'What is wrong?'

'That was Helga,' said Faro. 'Didn't you see her? She's just hurried towards the station exit.'

Dieter stared at him. 'It cannot be. She never boarded the train. I told you she left us at Paris to stay with her grandmother.'

'I tell you it was her.'

'You must be mistaken, many servants wear the same sort of outdoor garments as Helga. They are not unique by any means.'

The boys now wanted to know what had happened, what all the excitement was about. The three talked in rapid German, impossible for Faro to grasp and interpret.

As the whistle blew and the train began to move, Faro knew he was once again rendered helpless, in a situation he could do nothing about.

The train gathered speed and he sat back in his seat, frustrated and angry, certain that he had not been mistaken, that the woman he had seen was Helga. He was certain, also, that Dieter had seen her and lied. Otherwise, how could he describe what she was wearing? Faro hadn't described that to him.

Now the question was why? Why? Faro did not like being tormented by illogical reasons. His instinct would have been to race after the woman, who had always been an enigma, and question her. Her disappearance raised burning issues, in particular what she was doing on the train after all and why Dieter had lied about her staying in Paris if he was not somehow involved in the deception.

Seeing Helga again aroused one of those imponderables which had long intrigued Faro – the reason for her presence in the first place. At least knowing that she was still alive removed one of his hidden fears about her disappearance, that something more permanent than a digestive upset had removed her from the train. He was consoled that he could dismiss the sinister thoughts regarding her fate that had plagued him since they left Paris. But that did nothing to settle his growing suspicion that Helga might have been involved with the kidnappers at Glenatholl and, even more disturbingly, the fatal accident to George's bodyguard Tomas.

He tried to remember the man, who was certainly more lightly built than Dieter. Helga was a big strong woman, and as a servant would have had the most ready excuse for persuading Tomas that a window was jammed, and then pushing him out of it.

If that was so, then there was an undeniable link with the attempt to push Anton overboard on the ferry. She might have been pretending to sleep in the cabin and followed him out on deck. Faro remembered the boy's uncertainty, his exact words. 'Someone – I think it was a man – '

Such also had been the description of George's kidnapper. In neither case had the face of 'a big strong man' been seen. George was grabbed from behind, lifted bodily. In the darkness Anton saw only a shadowy figure, a stout stick raised to strike him. In the darkness big strong Helga could have been mistaken for a man by a frightened boy. And Faro also remembered George's idea that one of his kidnappers might have been a woman, since her footsteps were lighter.

Faro's thoughts were interrupted by the arrival of the *chef de train*. 'There was a telegraph message waiting for us at Strasbourg for Herr Dieter. We should have had it when we arrived in Paris but it came too late.'

Dieter read it and said to George, 'It is really for you, Highness. The Grand Duchess, your mother, is home again from Mosheim. She is safe and well and longing to see you.'

George took the telegraph and read it out to them again.

'Such good news,' said Dieter. 'Is it not?'

'May I see?' Faro asked. The message had been transmitted from Paris earlier that day to await arrival of the Orient Express at its next point of call. Unfortunately the time stamp was illegible.

George was delighted. 'I am so glad.'

Faro was having similar thoughts. He had been afraid that news might arrive that Amelie had died of her injuries in Germany. At this rate he might safely conclude that his journey, his royal command to restore George to his kingdom, would end when he saw the boy on to the Luxorian train at Stuttgart.

He was glad, relieved in fact. He had little desire to go into the home of Amelie and George. Some of this was self-preservation. He dreaded a meeting with the President, with a guilty feeling that if he were seen with George their unmistakable likeness might raise grave doubts in the President's mind about his own paternity. Gustav was not a man, by all accounts, who would take that kindly and Faro realised that the possibility of leaving Luxoria unscathed would be remote indeed. He would meet with an unfortunate accident, be eliminated. And George. Nor would President Gustav have any remaining scruples about Amelie.

It was a grim picture and Faro suspected that the secret was out already. Once or twice he had seen Dieter watching George and him with a curious expression. After seeing their reflections together in the compartment mirror opposite Faro avoided sitting next to the boy. Perhaps he was overreacting and his safety lay in the fact that Dieter would never imagine the Grand Duchess of Luxoria in an intimate relationship with a commoner. Especially an Edinburgh policeman.

94

Casting aside his gloomy thoughts and observing George, he was greatly consoled by the boy's joy and excitement at the prospect of being reunited with his mother. By a bitter twist of fate, he had unknowingly met his real father but their time together was brief, already almost over. The secret was safe, never to be revealed. Indeed, it was better for all concerned that they were unlikely ever to meet again.

The detective in Faro sighed. Already he was forced to mentally draw a line under Tomas's accident and Helga's disappearance, as well as George's kidnapping at Glenatholl. A few hours more and he would never know the answers to those unsolved mysteries. Although he had reached some conclusions, they would remain interesting theories only. It was very irritating, but he was aware that he had reached a dividing line and the time had arrived when he must set aside a lifetime's habit of thinking like a detective.

As Imogen often advised, he was too ready to make a crime out of the most innocent happening. 'After all,' she had said, 'the world is littered with unexplained things and weird coincidences.'

Faro was not convinced, believing that an explanation could be found for everything, if one looked hard enough. But the memory of Imogen's words made him smile. He would have a lot to tell her, so much to discuss about George and Glenatholl and the Orient Express.

Suddenly he was content to look ahead, glad to be embarking on the next stage of his journey. He had come to terms with the inevitability of parting with George. Once the Luxoria train departed with the boy in Dieter's care, he would send a wire to Imogen and be on his way to Heidelberg.

He had it all planned.

It was not to be.

15

Before sending a message to Imogen, Faro required a reliable timetable. No doubt this would be available at Stuttgart railway station.

When he mentioned this Dieter seemed pleased at the prospect of their journey's end and said, with more enthusiasm than usual, 'It is possible that the guard will have timetables since the Orient Express passengers often have to link up with other trains.'

'Good,' said Faro. 'I'll take a walk along the train. See if I can find some information about trains to Heidelberg.' He was feeling restless as well as in desperate need of exercise after all the rich fare he had consumed.

'May I come with you, sir?' asked George.

'Of course.'

'I should like to see the rest of the train.'

'Me too,' said Anton.

The two boys hurried ahead of Faro, chattering excitedly, while Dieter trailed in the rear.

Walking along the corridors they were greeted by other passengers similarly engaged in this very restricted activity, the only exercise available on the great train.

A door ahead of them opened and amid shrieks a tiny dog rushed out barking and dragging a ball of wool entangled in its paws. As the dog's owner appeared, shouting to it to stop, Faro stooped down, grabbed the little creature's collar and returned it to the middle-aged lady, who was volubly expressing her gratitude in German.

Suddenly he realised that the ball of wool was familiar. A ball of red knitting wool.

'That belonged to Helga!' he said sharply to Dieter.

Dieter said nothing, merely shook his head and gave a despairing sigh.

'I tell you that is her wool. Ask the lady where her dog got it from.'

'I cannot do that,' Dieter protested.

'Of course you can. Do it!'

There followed a conversation of what seemed like interminable argument and length. It was very difficult to follow but Faro gathered that the lady thought he wanted the wool for some reason and freed her pet from its entanglement, eager to hand it over.

Faro got only the gist of it. 'Ask her where her dog found it?'

The woman clearly thought this Englishman was quite mad and Dieter said, 'The dog has had it since before they left Paris, so it could not have belonged to Helga. She would never have been parted from her knitting.'

'She could have dropped it,' Faro insisted.

Dieter gave an exasperated sigh. 'Red is not an unusual colour, Mr Faro. Many women the length and breadth of Europe will be knitting garments in that colour. This is a mere coincidence. I should advise you to be calm, sir.'

Calm indeed! Here was Dieter making him sound like the village idiot. Damn!

Again that frustration of not knowing the language, but Faro was

97

sure the woman was pointing and saying that the dog had found it. Someone lost it. He heard the word Strasbourg. Left the train?

Certain that Dieter was lying, Faro groaned. If only George hadn't dashed ahead. He could have translated.

Finally, with a rather angry look in Faro's direction, the woman dismissed them and returned to her compartment, clutching the dog and firmly closing the door.

Aware of Dieter's long-suffering sigh, Faro knew there was nothing more he could do. The guard appeared and he asked for a timetable to Heidelberg. 'I do not have one, sir, but we will be arriving in Stuttgart shortly.'

Why should he care what had happened to Helga? He would never know anyway, since this journey on the fabulous Orient Express was almost over for him, something of a wasted experience, since he realised he would remember little but his own frustrations.

Ten minutes later they were approaching Stuttgart, gathering together their luggage, as they prepared to wait on the branch line where the Luxorian train would collect them.

A tap on the door announced the *chef de train*. 'Sirs, I have bad news,' he said, handing Dieter a piece of paper which he read, his face expressionless.

'What is it?' demanded Faro anxiously.

Dieter sighed. 'The storm we have come though has done widespread damage. There has been a landslide. The royal train will be delayed for a few hours until the line can be cleared.'

'I have a suggestion, sir,' said the *chef de train*, eager to be helpful.

'In English, if you please,' said Faro, determined not to miss any of this vital information.

'Yes, sir. About ten kilometres distant there is an alternative route. The old railway line to the Luxorian border which was closed as unnecessary when the Orient Express took over. It is now used only for freight trains.'

'And?' said Dieter.

'We pass by, a mere half kilometre from the old station. It would be possible to halt there and for you to disembark. It is just a short distance to walk over to the siding, which you will be able to see from the train.'

Dieter frowned, clearly put out by this new suggestion, and Faro decided that knowing even less about the terrain he had better keep his thoughts to himself. Dieter was leader of the party, decisions were in his hands.

'What sort of station facilities are there?' he asked.

'None, sir. It is no longer used. They need to keep the line open as the freight trains move a lot slower than our express train. There is a waiting-room, and a porter in attendance. It will be for only a very short time,' he added encouragingly.

As he was speaking the great train came to a halt. 'Over there, sir, you can see the siding.'

There had been a fall of snow and the black-and-white world, with a wood and a slight hill, was a very unappealing sight.

'It looks like the middle of nowhere,' whispered George.

It did indeed.

The siding had long since ceased to be dignified as a railway station. The Orient Express would have passed it by without being aware of its existence. The recent heavy snowfall did nothing to soften the bleak dreariness and isolation of a tiny hut alongside the platform, the waiting-room of the *chef de train's* somewhat extravagant description.

Steps were provided to set them down on the track.

The *chef de train* was full of apologies. He was very polite but, to anyone carefully observing his expression, hardly able to conceal his impatience to get his train safely under way again. And not only for the delays to his scheduled timetable, there was another much more important reason: safety.

And that was uppermost in his mind at this moment as he looked anxiously down the track at the lovely gleaming length of his train. He did not know the identity of the two boys, but guessed that the party must be important Luxorian nationals to be able to afford such a journey. He did not want trouble from some irate official in London, so he would make ample provision that they did not go hungry while they waited.

Beside their luggage, a large picnic hamper appeared. 'This with our compliments, sir. We hope it will make your waiting more pleasant.'

What the Luxorian nationals did not know, and the *chef de train* did not care to brood upon, was that this was a notorious area with greater dangers to life and limb than a heavy snowfall and going hungry for a few hours. There were brigands, notorious killers who would have shot a man for considerably less than the picnic hamper and a few pieces of luggage.

He was already looking over his shoulder as he talked, praying that this wild and apparently empty countryside would not suddenly erupt with whooping gun-firing horsemen, tempted to descend on his precious Orient Express by the prospect of so many treasures within their grasp. In this dangerous territory the freight trains carried guns and the guards went armed. On his train, so civilised and fashionable, there was nothing so vulgar as an armed guard, no soldiers with a gun-carriage at the ready. The thought of his passengers made him want to weep. The ladies, such wealth, such jewels. Such pickings.

Already conscious of illustrious countenances bearing irate looks staring out of windows and standing on the train's steps, demanding to know what the delay was all about, he realised he had lingered too long already. He looked at the little group with their luggage and the picnic basket. Two young boys, he thought sadly. Then he remembered he had daughters that age. Not privileged girls, but ones who would need good dowries.

Should he warn the two men of the possible dangers that lay ahead, just out of sight perhaps? If anything happened to his train he thought of all those other illustrious passengers who would would not hesitate to bring an action against La Companie Internationale. He shuddered, thinking of the tears and tirades of his wife, the miseries of his children should he be held responsible, brought before a company tribunal, down-graded or worse, dismissed.

No. He must not linger. And bowing quickly, he boarded the train and left their fate in God's hands. He hoped.

16

Faro watched the train disappear snail-like into the gathering nightfall, its smoke a series of pale exclamation marks against the darkening sky.

Left stranded by the empty railway line, he felt suddenly angry and resentful. Having seen George and Anton safely aboard the Luxorian train in the custody of Dieter, with a telegraph sent to Imogen, he should now be waiting on a platform in Stuttgart for the Heidelberg train. He looked in exasperation at the little group for which his responsibility was not yet ended, the two boys scared and vulnerable.

Faro considered the landscape with a jaundiced eye. As far as he could gather, they were the only humans visible in a desolate land, a world in mourning, where spring's rebirth was a forlorn hope in the wilderness which nature had forgotten.

At his side, Dieter wearily picked up the valise and the picnic hamper, the two boys having swiftly deserted the luggage and, waiting for someone to tell them what to do next, were pelting each other with snowballs.

'It will soon be dark,' said Dieter. 'We should get settled for the night. Delays in this area can be lengthy. We must not expect too much.'

'Then we had better see what the building over there can offer,' said Faro with little hope as they set off in the direction of the old railway siding.

They stumbled over the rough ground. The recent heavy snowfall, unmarked by human footfalls, might have appeared beautiful in any other context. Nothing, however, could soften the bleak dreariness of the landscape around them, broken by one solitary building. By no stretch of imagination could this small wooden hut be dignified as the waiting-room of the *chef de train*'s description, Faro thought grimly.

They pushed open the door. By a flickering stove, a dejected-looking porter with only a red and rather dripping nose visible above the swathe of shawls in which he was huddled against the cold, picked up a wavering lamp to inspect the new arrivals. Perhaps expecting an influx of would-be passengers, he went to the door and, peering into the gloom, he raised the lamp and shook his head by way of acknowledgement, since greeting seemed a gross exaggeration for that expression of woeful melancholy.

'The Luxorian train?' Cupping his hand to his ear, he answered Dieter's question and stared up and down the line. 'No, Excellencies, I have been told nothing about any engine from Luxoria. It is not on my station schedule,' he added sternly. 'We deal only with freight trains.'

Dieter resumed a detailed explanation in German which Faro gathered related to the landslide emergency. The porter clearly understood not one word but was intent on argument. Exasperated Dieter turned to Faro.

'This is getting us nowhere.' And turning back to the porter, 'Perhaps I can telegraph Luxoria and let them know that we are here and waiting for the train to collect us?'

The man shook his head triumphantly at that. 'No, Excellency, you cannot. For the simple reason that we don't have one. It broke down years ago and was never replaced.'

'Then where is the nearest office?'

'Two kilometres down the line.'

Dieter translated this new disaster briefly for Faro's benefit.

'I will go,' Dieter added finally. 'I must let them know where we are.'

'Let me come with you,' said Anton.

'No. You stay with Mr Faro. It isn't far and I will be back as soon as I can.'

Faro admired the man's courage. He did not fancy the inactivity of waiting but someone had to remain with the boys. He was painfully conscious of his limitations in this emergency, helpless to deal with the intricacies of sending telegraph messages in a language only half understood in a German zone with a difficult local dialect, if the porter was anything to judge by.

'There must be houses somewhere not too far off,' said George.

'What makes you think that?' asked Faro hopefully.

'When we were playing in the snow out there, we heard dogs barking, didn't we Anton?'

Dogs? Faro and Dieter exchanged anxious looks. Guessing that it was more likely the distant howl of a wolf pack, Faro followed the bodyguard outside. 'You will take care.'

Dieter looked towards the woods, a thick black impenetratable mass. 'Yes. But do not trouble yourself on my account. Wolves will not attack me. I will borrow the porter's lamp. Fire will keep them at bay. And I have a gun. I will be quite safe.'

'I think you should wait until daybreak.'

'And spend all night just waiting, doing nothing?' Dieter laughed harshly. Faro understood that this emotion was one they shared and any further argument was useless. With George and Anton, he watched Dieter walking down the track until the swinging lamp was swallowed up by the darkness.

Inside the tiny hut the two boys huddled close to the stove, while the old porter applauded his good fortune in sharing the travellers' hamper of excellent food. The only item which he recognised instantly being cold roast chicken. But his palate happily accommodated all the new tastes, the like of which he had never before experienced and had little hope of ever doing so again. And such wine too!

At last he bedded down on what was little more than a straw pallet in a corner farthest from the door. The comfort of the travellers was not his concern. Wrapping his voluminous cape around himself, he was soon snoring and Faro wondered if he had a home somewhere and what had brought an old man long past retirement age to such a comfortless existence.

Yawning, the two boys looked helplessly at Faro as he considered two long wooden benches facing each other on opposite walls in what must have been a cold and inhospitable waiting-room even in its better days. At least the porter had indicated that there were plenty of logs to keep the fire going all night, mostly old sleepers from a broken-down platform.

'We must be thankful for small mercies,' Faro told the boys, setting Anton to sleep on one bench and George on the other. 'We are well-fed and warm. We will survive until morning very well indeed.'

'Where will you sleep, sir?' asked George.

Faro indicated a wooden chair.

'You may have my bench, sir. I will sleep there.'

Faro smiled. 'Thank you for the offer, but as it is five feet long and I am over six feet tall, I think it is better adapted for your needs than mine.' He nodded towards the chair. 'I will do excellently in that.' He refrained from adding that he would not be able to sleep until he saw Dieter safely back.

And so he began his vigil. The two boys were silent, probably exhausted, and he hoped asleep for outside the barking they had mistaken for dogs became unmistakably wolves howling.

It grew noisier, hungrier and bolder. And nearer.

After a while, George sat up. 'I cannot sleep, Mr Faro. I am too excited. Seeing Mama tomorrow, I expect. I can hardly believe it. I am so glad to be going home again. I never realised it until now. I do wish you could meet my mother, sir. You would like her very much.'

Faro did not doubt that as he nodded politely.

'And she will like you and want to thank you for bringing me safely home.' Pausing he looked at the book open on Faro's knee. 'But I am disturbing you, sir. I have finished *Treasure Island*, I enjoyed it but real life is much more exciting, isn't it?'

Faro could only agree to that too. There were few moments in most boys' lives and he hoped, there would be none in this particular lad's existence, more exciting and dangerous than the present one of being stranded in an old railway-hut with a starving wolf pack howling outside the door.

'I should like to read more books by Mr Stevenson,' said George. 'Has he written anything else I might like and find interesting?'

Faro did not think there were many books more exciting and interesting than *Kidnapped* which had a curious parallel in George's life and his own at this very moment.

'It is the story of a man and a boy on a terrific adventure and the friendship that grew between them in danger. Mr Stevenson, someone wrote, had a genius for friendship. And he knew what he was talking about, he has a young stepson.'

'I should like to read that book, sir.'

'Then I shall send you a copy as soon as I get back to Scotland.'

'Oh, thank you, sir. I shall look forward to that.'

'Some of their adventures are in the Highlands. You'll enjoy that part, I'm sure.'

George sighed sadly. 'And I will keep it to remind me of my time at Glenatholl.' He looked at Faro. 'I do wish I had the chance to see your islands, Mr Faro, your Orkney.'

'So you shall when you come to Britain again.'

But he knew, and he thought that George also knew, how remote the possibility was of his return to school or even to Scotland in the foreseeable future.

George looked at him. 'I would be greatly obliged, sir, if you would tell me a little more about the Vikings.'

'I will gladly.'

And so, by the embers of a dying stove that cracked and sparked as Faro fed it more logs, with George at his side, he retold stories from the *Orkneyinga Saga* of the Norse chieftains, of Vikings and trolls and mermaids.

And of how his own grandmother was reputed to be a seal woman. 'She had webbed toes and fingers and people said she had magic powers of foretelling the future. She came from the kingdom of the sea, so folks believed.'

George listened enthralled as Faro told him the legend of the seal woman, not his grandmother this time, one who was taken in a fisherman's net and, falling in love with her captor, shed her skin and became mortal. They married and had children. Then one day she found, hidden in an old chest, her seal skin. When she took it in her hands, the sea called her home again.

He looked down at George, his head resting against his shoulder. He was breathing deeply, fast asleep and Faro pushed back his hair and kissed his forehead gently. As he did so he whispered in his heart the words he must never utter aloud, 'Goodnight, my son – my dear son.'

As he was settling him on the bench, George opened his eyes momentarily, sighed and with a shiver closed his eyes again. Faro, fearing that he was chilled, threw his Ulster coat over him and returned to his wooden chair and Edwin Drood.

With so many mysteries of his own since he had begun the book, he found his concentration wandering.

Where was Dieter? Why was he taking so long?

Determined to keep vigil, to stay awake until he returned, he read a few more pages.

Sleep seemed impossible as the old porter's snores deadened even the wolves' hungry howling outside the door.

17

Sometime around daybreak, Faro awoke from a bad dream. For a moment he had not the least idea where he was, then every aching bone in his body reminded him that he had spent the night sitting upright on a hard wooden chair.

The faint light from the window revealed that the two boys still slept and the porter snored as gustily as ever.

But Dieter had not returned.

The fire was dead ashes, the room bitterly cold, and ice had formed on the window pane clouded by the sleepers' breaths.

Faro opened the door and walked along the snowy platform. Animal pawmarks everywhere indicated that the wolves had been very active, hungrily pacing back and forth outside the door.

He shuddered. Why had Dieter failed to return? What had become of him? Faro stared down the track in the direction the man had taken, certain now that he could not have survived. He had fallen victim to the wolves or some other dire misfortune.

Faro shook his head sadly, full of sudden remorse never having thought it possible that he would long to see the man he had instinctively disliked. And, it now appeared, quite irrationally distrusted.

Obviously the personality of a killer also had in it the necessary thread of fierce courage required to face the inevitable. This was no new discovery for Faro. In a lifetime of dealing with hardened criminals he'd often found that no man is totally evil. The human soul has its redemption clause.

He walked back into the hut, a haven in comparison with the hostile landscape outside. The porter, still swathed as he had slept, was already relighting the fire, grumbling to himself as he did so.

The boys had awakened and announced that they were very hungry. As they went outside to relieve themselves, George said cheerily, 'Come along, Anton, remember the rules in Glenatholl. We would have been ordered in the absence of water to use the snow to wash our face and hands.'

They did not linger over their ablutions and returned indoors shivering as Faro opened the picnic hamper. He had not expected it to have to last another day and was glad to see that the contents had been generous and there was still bread and cheese remaining from the night before.

Strangely, perhaps because of his hidden fears, he wasn't hungry and settled for coffee, which the old porter brewed up on his spirit stove.

'Where is Dieter?' asked George anxiously. 'We must save something for him. Shouldn't he be back by now, sir?'

Faro tried to sound casual and reassuring. 'I expect he decided it was safer to stay near the telegraph office until daylight.'

'You mean because of the wolves?' asked George quietly.

Faro looked at him.

'We saw their footprints outside, a whole pack, by the look of them.' He sounded scared and Faro realised that he had under-estimated the boys' imaginations. Dogs, indeed!

'I imagine Dieter thought it was too dangerous to walk back in the dark. Perhaps he had to wait until the telegraph office reopened this morning to send his message. I expect he'll arrive any minute now with the train. Just think, this time tomorrow you will both be waking up in your own beds,' he added with a confidence he was far from feeling.

He smiled at Anton, silent, asking no questions, curiously withdrawn from their anxiety about Dieter. And watchful. Watchful was an odd word to use for the boy's complete lack of emotion, which had concerned Faro in the earlier part of the journey and now worried him more than ever. After all, Dieter was his bodyguard, which suggested that his standing in Luxoria must warrant such an appointment.

As for George, he regarded Faro with an expression of faint disbelief. And no wonder. The boy could count and the train that should have been with them last night was now ten hours late.

As for himself, he was feeling the full force of the predicament of being in a foreign country in an area where his basic knowledge of German, which he had been at pains to keep concealed, was utterly useless, too basic to deal with any emergencies.

He looked despairingly at these two boys – fourteen and twelve and he was entirely responsible for seeing them safely to Luxoria. Not in his wildest dreams had such an idea presented itself.

As the boys finished eating and rushed out to play in the snow, he watched from the window, afraid to let them out of his sight for a moment. The porter smoked a fierce pipe and totally ignored these unwelcome sharers of his hut's hospitality.

Another hour ticked by and still Dieter did not appear, nor did any trains. Occasionally the distant noise of an engine had them alert and listening, rushing to the door, only to watch with considerable frustration the passage of an express train thundering down the main line.

Faro had come to a decision. If by the end of the day neither the Luxorian train nor Dieter had put in an appearance then he would have to try to find some way to get himself and the boys to Stuttgart. He hoped for some inspiration, that some bright idea would come to him of how one stops an express train without endangering the safety of the passengers or getting killed in the process.

Then suddenly he heard it. A sound from far off, but not in the direction of the express trains. This one was coming from over the hill.

A train's engine?

He listened, and saw the boys look up from the wooden board they had turned into a sledge and were using on a snowy mound.

'The train – the train – at last.'

'No.' Not a train. Rifle shots.

The porter appeared at the door, shouted something incomprehensible to Faro and waved urgently to the two boys. Whatever he said, they needed no second bidding and raced through the snow to the hut. The porter pulled them quickly inside and closed the door. He was trembling.

George turned to Faro. 'He says it is not the train. It is the brigands.'

Brigands. Dear God.

If confirmation was needed the rifle shots were nearer now, mingled with the sound of horses, and yells and shouts which made the wolves' howling during the night an attractive alternative.

The porter was speaking to George again.

'Translate?' Faro demanded.

'He says they are like buzzards watching for carrion. They will have been watching us and know how few we are. They must have seen us leaving the train yesterday, saw our luggage – guessed there would be rich pickings.'

Faro wanted to ask why they had waited so long. Why didn't they attack during the night? George continued to translate the porter's terror into English.

'When the Luxorian train didn't arrive, they must have guessed we were stranded.'

Faro glared at the porter and put a finger to his lips indicating that he had said enough. He didn't want the boys to be any more terrified.

George looked scared. 'What will happen to us?' he asked Faro.

'We two will be all right,' Anton put in quickly. 'No harm will come to us. We will be taken hostage.' He put a comforting arm around George's shoulders. 'They don't kill children and we will be valuable to them. Not like adults.'

This was the first comment Anton had made and Faro realised he meant well although his remark clearly indicated that Faro need not expect to be so fortunate.

As for hostages, they might well be valuable to the brigands but not quite as Anton believed.

For one thing, they would have no idea of the importance of the two boys, that one was heir to the kingdom of Luxoria. Brigands did not move in the circles of diplomacy, or know anything of subtle bargaining with royal households.

Faro shook his head. He would die fighting, but no one could have any doubt of the fate of two well-grown boys if they were captured, or of the naivety of Anton's words. They would not be killed, since two strong healthy boys were useful to boost the brigands' numbers and fighting strength, which was frequently depleted by running battles. Rifles would be thrust into their hands and they would be told how to use them and made to fight alongside the brigands. There were other unpleasant things likely to happen to Anton and George among such men that Faro preferred not to think about.

The shouts, din of horses and rifle shots indicated that they were close at hand.

'What do we do, sir?' asked George, biting his lip but trying to sound brave.

'We fight them off, of course,' said Faro.

'But there are only three of us,' said Anton.

'And one with a gun,' said Faro grimly, producing the revolver he had never expected to use.

The porter who saw his action grinned and gave a crow of

delight. From under his voluminous cape he produced a rifle and waved it vigorously.

Saluting Faro he said to George, 'I had the honour to serve in the Imperial Army of the Kaiser fighting the French when I was a lad.'

George translated and said, 'If anything happens to either of you, I can use a rifle. I learned how when I was at Balmoral with the shooting party last year,' he added in casual tones. And with an apologetic smile at Anton, 'Sorry that you didn't get the chance as well, but you were just with the beaters.'

Normally Faro's eyes would have widened at the idea of an eleven-year-old using a rifle on the grouse moors. How soon did the royals begin teaching their young the art of slaying wild animals!

But there was not a moment to lose. The shots and yells were outside. The platform vibrated and the little hut shook to its foundations with the sound of horses' hooves.

Faro's last thought before he went into action was of the Four Horsemen of the Apocalypse.

Was this what it was like to die?

18

Telling the boys to lie down on the floor well out of range of window and door, Faro broke the window with his revolver, took careful aim and cheered as one of the brigands gave a groan of pain and slumped in the saddle.

The platform cleared instantly. But surely one wounded man was not enough to scare them off.

Cautiously Faro looked out of the window again. Gathered at a little distance a group of twelve horsemen were drawn up together. They were not quite as he had pictured a band of villainous desperados. There was a military precision about the group despite the red bandanas tied around their foreheads. Their horses, no motley collection of stolen animals, had the sleek well-groomed look of regimental steeds.

As he watched, the men were gathered around one man, conferring or awaiting instructions. The leader suddenly emerged and rode forward swiftly towards the hut, alone and carrying on his rifle a white flag.

'A flag of truce!' yelled George. 'We are saved!'

He ran forward but Faro stopped him. 'Wait. I'll go first. You translate for me, George.'

As he opened the door, the horseman with his white flag rode on to the platform. He did not dismount.

He looked at George, his expression puzzled for a moment, then at Anton who was standing close behind him.

'You – ' he pointed. 'You boy – '

Anton stepped forward.

'Come here!'

Anton went over to the man, head up, and Faro marvelled at his bravery. The man leaned over, said something inaudible and seizing Anton around the waist lifted him bodily on to the horse.

Anton stared back at them, bewildered, and Faro guessed too terrified even to protest, to cry out.

'Anton! Anton!' George screamed as he watched his friend being carried back to the group. Then to Faro and the porter who was watching open-mouthed, 'Don't you see, they're taking him hostage. Why didn't either of you kill that man? You could have at least taken a shot at him,' he sobbed.

Faro did not reply. He was watching the group, already riding fast, disappearing across the hill. Then he said gently to George:

'You know we couldn't do that. We have to honour the white flag and if we had fired, we might have hit Anton, or they might have killed him in revenge.' He put his arm around the still sobbing George.

'Dieter will be back shortly. He will know what to do.'

It was little consolation and he didn't believe his own words. Neither did George.

'He isn't coming back,' George said shortly. 'I think Dieter is dead.'

There was nothing more Faro could say. At that moment, he too was certain that they had seen the last of Dieter.

Still with an arm about George's shoulders he led him back into the hut. The boy was trembling, his face white with fear, but trying to keep his voice calm, he asked: 'What will we do now, Mr Faro. What is to become of us?'

115

Faro had no answer to that. But there were a lot of questions that required answers. There were things in this particular puzzle, this dire and dreadful adversary which was death itself, questions with answers that did not make any sense at all.

He simply had to think. And fast. Because whatever the nature of those horsemen who had taken Anton hostage, time was running out. If George was to survive to reach Luxoria, there was not a moment to lose.

Inside, the porter was gathering together his few possessions. Waving his arms about, he shouted to George and ushered them outside. As they watched he seized their luggage, dragged it outside and locked the door of the hut, turning on them a face of furious indignation.

Faro began to protest but George translated. 'It's no use, sir. He says he's an old man and he's not going to be at the mercy of brigands. He has never experienced anything like this before, they have always left him alone and now he is not prepared to risk his life. He is going back to his village, four kilometres away, and the railway can find a younger man to deal with their freight trains and be shot at.'

It was quite a speech and the old man strode off without another word or a backward glance, leaving them helpless beside their forlorn pile of luggage.

Faro looked at the railtrack winding away into nowhere. The landscape was empty, but somehow menacing. The brigands had vanished, yet he felt the prickle of unease, an intuition that he knew better than to ignore, that the danger was by no means over.

Death was close at hand.

'Pick up your bag, George.'

'I'll carry Anton's,' said George. 'I can't leave it behind.'

Faro tested the weight. It wasn't heavy. 'I'll take it,' he said and with little idea where their next meal would be coming from, he gathered the remaining food from the picnic hamper.

'Now let's get away from here.'

As he started off down the line, George asked, 'Where are we going, sir?'

'We'll head towards the telegraph office, find out about trains.'

'Shouldn't we wait for a while, just in case – '

In answer a violent explosion split the air behind them. Faro threw George to the ground and sheltered him with his body.

The great whirlwind of noise was followed by an eerie silence. Cautiously Faro raised his head. Where the hut had been there was only a mass of shattered smoking timber.

'Someone blew it up, Mr Faro,' George gasped in a shocked frightened voice. 'We might have been inside.'

Faro regarded the ruin grimly. 'That, I think, was the general idea.'

'It wasn't the porter, surely. He seemed such a nice old man.'

'No. It wasn't the porter.'

'But he must have known.'

'He didn't, George. He wouldn't have put our luggage outside and locked the door if he'd known the place was going to blow up.'

'But how? Who?'

Gazing anxiously at the horizon, Faro said, 'Let's keep going. We shouldn't linger, in case they come back to inspect the damage.'

Seizing the bags, he walked rapidly down the line.

'Was it an accident, sir, do you think?' George asked hopefully.

When Faro shook his head, he said: 'You think it was the brigands. It was as well they got Anton out first.'

Faro stopped in his tracks and said 'Exactly, George. And that, I am afraid, was the plan. We were the target – and the old man, if he had been foolish enough to stay around.'

'What will they do to Anton now?'

'I don't think we need worry too much about Anton. Nothing is going to happen to him.'

'But they kidnapped him. He'll be a hostage.'

They had been walking for some time before Faro decided it was safe to stop by a curve in the railway line, well out of sight of the pile of rubble that had been once been a railway waiting-room.

There were some boulders by the side of the track and Faro said, 'Let's sit down here for a moment.'

George sighed. 'I don't understand, Mr Faro. We both saw that man with the white flag come and take Anton.' He shook his head. 'We saw it with our own eyes – '

Faro remembered that well-dressed, smartly turned-out band of brigands with their fine horses and military precision.

'They kidnapped him, sir. Took him hostage,' George continued.

'That, I'm afraid, is what we were meant to think. Think back, George, were you near enough to hear what the man said to Anton as he lifted him on to the horse?'

George shrugged. 'I thought he was telling him not to be afraid – that all would be well. Something like that.'

'Exactly. Nice soothing words. Not quite what one would expect from a savage blood-thirsty brigand.'

George thought for a moment. 'Actually, he had quite a nice voice, sir. Well-bred, you know.'

Faro nodded grimly. 'And I would have expected Anton to struggle more and for the man to be a little more convincing, rougher in dragging away a frightened and unwilling victim.'

George didn't answer and Faro continued, 'That wasn't the way you reacted with your kidnappers at Glenatholl, was it now?'

George shook his head. 'No. I fought and kicked and struggled.' Wide-eyed he stared at Faro. 'You mean – you mean, it was all pretend?'

'I'm pretty sure of that.'

'But why did they do it then? And what will they do with Anton?'

'That, my lad, is what I want you to tell me.'

'I don't understand.'

'I want you to tell me everything you know about Anton. Who is he for instance, this vague cousin who was sent to Glenatholl as your companion.'

George was silent for a moment, then he shrugged. 'I'm not

118

supposed to tell anyone, ever.' He looked up at Faro. 'You see, Anton is actually my half-brother.'

'Your *what?*'

'Yes, our father is President Gustav, but we have different mothers.'

At last, thought Faro, a lot of things were becoming clear, not exactly crystal, but well on the way.

So Anton was the President's natural son, the boy who had been an infant when Amelie came to Edinburgh, childless. His mother was the President's mistress, the reason why he wanted rid of Amelie, to marry her . . . And declare their son Anton legitimate. The heir to Luxoria.

'Well, well,' he said and George stared at him when he burst out laughing.

'Are you pleased, sir?' George smiled. 'He really is very nice when you get to know him. And he is very fond of me. He has always behaved just like an older brother should. Protective, you know.'

Faro thought grimly that there wasn't much protectiveness about leaving his little brother in a hut to be blown to smithereens. If, that was, he had known in advance what was in store for them from the so-called brigands.

But although knowing Anton's real identity at least provided some of the answers to the questions that had been plaguing him, it still didn't provide any ideas about what they should do next. And worst of all was the certain knowledge that his German wasn't up to coping with this particular kind of situation.

As if George had read his thoughts, he said, 'When we reach the telegraph office, sir, I am going to send a wire to Uncle Karl – he is Mama's most trusted servant and he will have returned to Luxoria with her. He has lots of influence with people who can help.'

'He is not her equerry?' asked Faro sharply, remembering the first victim of the assassin who, according to Sir Julian Arles, had taken the bullet meant for Amelie.

If that loyal servant was dead, then their last hope was indeed gone.

19

George laughed. 'Oh no, sir, Uncle Karl is much higher than that. He is a statesman as well as a soldier. He holds the rank of colonel in the Kaiser's Death's Head Hussars.'

'Is he also one of your President's men?' Faro could not bear to say 'father'.

'No,' said George firmly. 'He hates him because he has been very unkind to my mother, you know,' he added with a candour well beyond his years.

Faro did know, but his eyebrows raised a bit at hearing that piece of intelligence from the boy who believed the President to be his father.

'But Uncle Karl – Count Karl zu Echlenberg,' he added proudly. 'will make sure the train comes for us. And that we are safe.'

Faro had already taken that missing train into his calculations. Seen in the light of the last twenty-four hours' events, the landslide excepted – if that piece of information could be trusted – had there ever been any intention of sending the royal train? He could see the President's hand clearly directing the whole operation, the ambush at the railway merely a device to rescue Anton, his own son, and destroy Amelie's child.

Faro had little doubt that the plan had been worked out well in advance. Starting with the Grand Duchess Amelie's assassination while she was in Germany, the trap was then laid for George to be summoned home from Britain, and annihilated before he reached the frontier in an unfortunate accident!

Faro himself, whom the President had never heard of, as well as any other appointed bodyguards of George, would be regarded as expendable.

The plan was emerging clearly now.

After a brief time of national mourning, President Gustav would marry his mistress, Anton's mother, and take over dictatorship of Luxoria, declaring their son as the next heir.

Even an unskilled politician like Faro could recognise that this was not only a personal vendetta, but behind it was the fact that Kaiser Wilhelm II was a long-term friend and supporter of the Grand Duchess and, what was vastly more important, he wished to bring Luxoria under the vast and ever-growing umbrella of Imperial Germany.

When Faro had agreed under duress to Her Majesty's request that he see her goddaughter's son back to Luxoria, he had done so without the least suspicion that the move was involved in international politics. A situation from which he would have instinctively recoiled, remote from any he encountered during his duties as a detective with the Edinburgh City Police, this was a development beyond his wildest nightmares or experience.

Realising the enormity of his personal involvement, he was tempted to blink rapidly, as he did in bad dream, a technique he had perfected in childhood to wake himself up. Alas for his hopes that he would open his eyes and breathe a sigh of relief, find that it had all gone away and he was back in his comfortable bed in Sheridan Place. That was the dream, but this was cold reality.

Here he was, sitting by a railway track, a foreigner in a strange land, with him a twelve-year-old prince, the heir to a kingdom, whose safety was entirely in his hands and whose real identity he must never reveal, much as he longed to shout out the truth.

He looked at the boy. They were both cold and hungry, prey to wolves and the President's secret army who would hunt them down once they knew that they had survived the explosion.

That vital link with the world of sanity and safety, the telegraph office, still lay far down the railway track somewhere out in that desolate landscape, haphazardly dotted with sticks of dead-looking trees and boulders that a little imagination might turn into crouching brigands. They could have been sitting on Mars, Faro thought, but for the occasional very distant and frustrating emblem of civilisation, an express train thundering into Germany, towards Frankfurt and Heidelberg. And Imogen Crowe.

While he wondered sadly if he had seen Imogen for the last time, he told George encouragingly not to worry.

'I have been in worse situations than this,' he said cheerfully.

'Have you really, sir?' asked George.

And Faro was glad he was not called upon to name one. At that precise moment he would have found it difficult even to remember anything of greater peril. True, he had fought villains in plenty in his long career. But on his own territory, where he made the rules; where he knew the terrain and the language; where people understood him and his requests to official channels were dealt with promptly; where Chief Inspector Faro was respected, obeyed. But here in this alien land Chief Inspector Faro did not exist. Here he was merely Mr Faro, a retired policeman who nobody knew, escorting the heir of Luxoria to his home.

George leaned against him, trying hard to be brave and not to shiver. Pretending not to notice, Faro produced the bread and cheese. They were in deadly peril, but as Faro sat with his arm around George's thin shoulders, he knew that, in the seemingly unlikely event of his survival, this was the memory he would take out and treasure every day for the rest of his life.

George ate hungrily. If this was a dreadful ordeal for himself, Faro thought, how much worse for a lad who had been protected and cosseted all his short life and had always been quite clear about where his next meal was coming from? A lad who had never faced anything more threatening than a badly-thrown cricket ball in Scotland and had just survived a well-directed bomb.

'I suppose I had better get used to things like that,' said George through a mouthful of bread, nodding back the way they had come, where the acrid fumes of gunpowder still lingered in the air.

'There is a lot of it about in Germany just now, don't you think?' he added with that curious way of seeming to know what was going on in Faro's mind.

Faro stood up, dusted down the crumbs and gathered the valises. 'We had better not be too sorry for ourselves and get to that telegraph office before we start getting hungry again,' he said, watching George wrap a piece of bread and cheese in a rather grey-looking handkerchief.

'No need to keep that – eat it if you can.'

George looked at it longingly and shook his head. 'I would like to, sir, very much. I could eat a horse as we say at Glenatholl. But I think I'll save it, just in case.'

'I'm sure we won't need it. We'll be seeing that telegraph office any minute. It can't be far away now,' Faro said encouragingly.

They had walked only a further hundred yards when they heard a sound. Not a train's distant vibration, but the sound of hooves – and close by.

'The brigands,' whispered George.

Worse than brigands, thought Faro, trained soldiers with orders to kill.

Looking round for cover, he seized George and dived behind the very inadequate shelter of a dismal-looking shrub.

They waited. The hoofbeats drew nearer . . .

'Listen!' said Faro.

'There's only one of them,' whispered George.

'And I think I can deal with that,' said Faro grimly. With more confidence than he felt, he took out his revolver and prayed that he did not miss, knowing that he had only a few bullets left.

The rider approached and Faro prepared to take aim.

A voice screamed at them.

'George! Mr Faro!'

'Anton!'

And George leapt out of his hiding-place as Anton jumped down from the horse.

The two boys embraced.

'Thank God you are safe,' said Anton and there was no need for translation of that into English.

'I thought you were both dead.'

Anton brushed his tear-filled eyes.

Faro stared in amazement, for he had never thought the lad capable of such emotion, or indeed, of any emotion at all.

'How did you escape?' asked George.

Surprises weren't over for Faro, as Anton's next move was even more out of character. He dropped on one knee, seized George's hand and said, 'Highness, you are my liege lord as well as my half-brother. I am your faithful servant until death. That I do most solemnly swear. Before this man,' he nodded towards Faro, 'who is a witness to my oath of allegiance.'

And George placed his hands upon Anton's head as one day, God willing, he would do in the Cathedral at Luxoria.

Anton stood up. The solemn moment was past. He dusted down his already grubby knees and looking suddenly rather self-conscious, he tied his horse's reins to a tree stump and in a breathless voice said, 'Do you mind if I sit down for a moment?'

George took out his handkerchief, and shook out the bread and cheese.

'I saved this for you – just in case.'

'Thank you. I'm so hungry.'

As Anton seized it and started munching gratefully, Faro,

regarding this curious scene, felt as if it was suddenly out of context. Their little trio had been miraculously removed from sudden death by a railway track in an outlying district of Stuttgart but if he blinked suddenly, he felt he would find himself instead witnessing the aftermath of a cricket match in the grounds of Glenatholl College. He groaned inwardly. What would he not have given for that to be true.

As for what still lay ahead, he dared not even try to imagine.

20

Watching Anton approvingly as he demolished the last crumbs, George said, 'We were so worried about you. We thought you were being held to ransom, didn't we, Mr Faro?'

'How did you manage to escape?' Faro asked. 'And with such a splendid horse.'

Anton sighed. 'I might as well tell you both the truth.'

'What do you mean, the truth?' demanded George.

'That I never was in any danger really. It just had to look that way, as if I was being taken hostage.' Biting his lip to hold back the tears he turned to Faro and said, 'You have no idea, sir.'

'I think I have,' said Faro. 'George said that he thought the man who seized you whispered to you that you were not to be afraid.'

'That is true,' said George. 'That was what the brigand leader said, wasn't it?'

'That is what he said.' Anton shook his head. 'But they were not brigands.'

'I realised that,' said Faro. 'They were soldiers, weren't they?'

'Yes.' Anton stared at him in amazement. 'Members of my father

'– I mean, the President's private army. I recognised a few of them, a crack regiment.'

Faro remembered the sleek horses and the red bandanas that had struck a false note as Anton continued: 'It was all set up to – ' he paused and looked anxiously at George,

' – to save me. When I heard that they had planted a bomb under the rubbish at the railway hut as they rode in to get me – ' he gulped and took a deep breath.

'It was meant to kill you, George. And Mr Faro and the porter too, I was horrified. I knew I had to warn you before it was too late. They had no idea that I knew what they intended, they had even given me a horse.'

Pausing, he looked at them and laughed proudly. 'They didn't expect me to try to escape and thought that a boy would be delighted to have such an excellent horse, be proud to ride with them.'

'Have you any idea where they were heading?' Faro asked. 'Where they were taking you?'

Anton shook his head. 'I think they were there only to escort me to the royal train. It is on its way here now.'

That, at least, sounded hopeful, thought Faro as George cheered.

'I rode like the wind back to that horrible hut,' Anton continued. 'When I was still quite far off I heard the explosion, my horse was terrified and after trying unsuccessfully to unseat me, he tried to bolt. But I got him under control. I thought I must have lost the way then I saw – saw all that was left of where we had stayed, just those smoking ruins.'

He looked at them both as if he still couldn't believe his eyes and then clenching his fists he buried his head in his hands for a moment. 'You can't imagine how I felt. It was dreadful, dreadful, the worst moment in my whole life.'

Turning, he looked at Faro. 'I am sorry, sir, you must think me an awful cry-baby but I really thought you were all dead. I had to steel myself to search for – for – well, you know – '

He shuddered at the memory. 'Then I started shouting, kept on shouting your names over and over, in case, by a miracle, any of you were still alive among the ruins. It seemed like hours later when I realised that if you weren't under – all that – then you must have got out in time. And you'd be walking down the track towards the telegraph office.'

He grinned. 'And I was right. Here you are. Safe!'

Safe! Perhaps, but for how long, thought Faro, seeing the two boys beaming with delight.

Personally he wouldn't put too much hope in the chances of safety until the moment that elusive Luxorian train put in an appearance and he saw the two boys delivered into safe hands and on their way home. Only then could he relax and think of the next stage of his own journey.

'What about Dieter?' George was asking.

Again Anton shook his head. 'I don't know. I don't know if he's even alive. They certainly haven't killed him or captured him because when I asked, they just shook their heads and said nothing. I thought, it might even be that he is in the plot to – to – ' He shrugged. 'He would never have told me, because he knew I would never agree to anything if he intended hurting George.' And turning to Faro, he said impulsively; 'Or you, sir. You have been so good to us on the journey. You've thought of everything. You're kind to George too.'

He took a deep breath. 'The other night, when I was supposed to be sleeping,' he said shyly, 'I was listening to you telling George that story about an island where you once lived. I knew whatever happened you would never let any harm come to him. Or to me. Although I was sometimes afraid that you had guessed, sir.'

'Guessed?' asked Faro.

'Yes, sir. You know, about that business on the ferry crossing,' he said shamefacedly.

'I thought it very unlikely,' said Faro but did not add that it had opened up an interesting new line of thought. 'Now if you are ready, shall we start walking again?'

Picking up his valise, George said in shocked tones, 'Are you telling us, Anton, that it was all lies? About being attacked and someone trying to throw you overboard.'

Anton sighed wearily. 'Dieter told me to do it. He said it was a practical joke, just to give Mr Faro something to think about.'

'He certainly did that,' said Faro acidly as George gasped, 'A practical joke! I don't think that was very funny.'

Anton shrugged. 'Dieter thought Mr Faro having been a detective might have worked one or two things out – '

'Like George's kidnapping at Glenatholl?' asked Faro and when Anton nodded cautiously, 'There were some curious things about your story, Anton. Your version of witnessing the incident didn't quite tie up with George's account. You said you saw him talking to a man you described as gypsy-looking but George told me no one spoke to him.' He paused to let that sink in. 'You realise there was a very good reason for that.'

Anton frowned as Faro went on. 'You know perfectly well what I'm saying. If George's so-called kidnappers had spoken then he might have recognised voices which were very familiar to him. Particularly yours.'

Anton shook his head. 'There never was a kidnapping attempt really.'

'You mean – you and Dieter arranged it all between you?' George interrupted. 'What a beastly thing to do, Anton.'

'I didn't much like it but Dieter persuaded me. He said it just had to look that way so you'd be sent back to Luxoria. He had been told that the President believed you would be in danger if you remained in Scotland. He thought it was a brilliant idea, especially after Tomas's accident. When I protested, he told me there had been an attempt on your mother's life, here in Germany but that I must not tell you because you would be terrified.'

'Was it true, about Mama?' George put in sharply.

He sounded panic-stricken and Faro said, 'You have the message from her, from the train.'

George sighed with relief. 'Of course. Of course.' His face darkened suddenly. 'What really happened to Tomas? Did Dieter push him out of the window?'

'I think perhaps he did, although he never admitted it.'

'But why should be – or anyone – do such a thing to Tomas?' George demanded.

'I imagine the reason was that he was afraid you were in some real danger that you knew nothing about,' said Faro.

'Dieter planned the kidnapping,' Anton explained. 'He told me that it was the President's wish and that he would be very angry if I did not obey.' Anton stopped and looked at Faro questioningly.

'Yes, Anton. Mr Faro knows – I've told him that we are half-brothers.' George shook his head, bewildered, as Anton said, 'I still cannot believe it. A father wanting to murder one of his own sons. It is just too awful. How could any father do such a thing?'

To Faro, however, the answer was grimly obvious. The secret was out. President Gustav had somehow found out the truth, and knew that George was not his child. It explained a great deal and put both George and himself – if he and the President ever had the misfortune to meet – in deadly peril.

George had returned to the Glenatholl incident. 'Something that puzzled me was that I seemed to recognise the footsteps of the other kidnapper. Now I realise why they were familiar. They were yours, Anton.'

'I am truly sorry.' And Anton sounded very repentant. 'But I have now taken the oath of fealty before a witness,' he nodded towards Faro. 'And I have promised to serve you loyally and never lie to you again.'

Anton's account had fitted some of the pieces together, but for Faro there were still unanswered gaps. Had it really been necessary to make George appear to be in deadly danger so that he could be withdrawn from Glenatholl and returned to Luxoria to be disposed of in his own country?

Perhaps that was only the most logical reason if his mother the Grand Duchess was no longer alive. But according to the telegraph message received on the train, she was alive and well and waiting for George in Luxoria.

'What about Helga?' Faro asked. 'Was she a part of Dieter's plot too?'

Anton shook his head. 'I don't know anything about her. Honestly, sir, I wasn't even aware of her at college. We never associated with the servants, of course. I don't remember seeing her and she wasn't very friendly, was she? She didn't want to talk to us or play cards on the journey to Paris.'

'She certainly did not look like a person with a fever, either,' remarked George the observant. 'She looked quite stout and healthy.'

'Do you know, I thought that too,' said Anton. 'And as she was going to Germany, it did seem odd that she left us in Paris,' He frowned. 'Unless she knew something from Dieter. Something he had told her or wanted her to do for him.'

'It could be that she was to send the wire to the Orient Express in Strasbourg,' said George, voicing the dire possibility occupying the forefront of Faro's mind. 'But Mr Faro was certain he saw her leaving the train there.'

'I might have been mistaken,' said Faro who had no wish for George to continue on his own grim line of thought that the wire from his mother was a fake. 'I only saw Helga's back view. I didn't see her face and as Dieter pointed out, perhaps quite rightly, a lot of servants wear the same sort of clothes.'

'Maybe she went to find out about the missing train – ' George began.

'Listen!'

A faint sound far off, growing steadily nearer.

What was this? A new danger? That fear was clearly visible in the scared looks the two boys exchanged.

21

Under their feet the track began to vibrate. Distant puffs of steam and there, a hundred yards down the line, a train was fast approaching.

They waved. The driver saw them, and blew on the whistle. Never had a sight been more welcome to Faro and the two boys than that of the engine of the State Railway of Luxoria as it braked to a halt.

Of more modest proportions and considerably less impressive than the Orient Express, the Luxorian engine was painted in the national colours and bore the royal flag. With a tall stove-pipe chimney in highly polished brass as well as the usual pipes, tubes and valves, exterior cylinders and brass-rimmed wheel-splashers, its open cab had a tiny roof which housed the driver and fireman in a space so small as to seem totally inadequate against the elements.

The head of the State Railways, in full ceremonial uniform, leapt down from the front carriage and bowed low to George. 'Welcome home, Your Highness.'

Acknowledging the man's greeting, George whispered gleefully to Faro: 'We're safe, safe – ' sounding as if he couldn't quite believe it.

Their luggage stowed aboard, Anton gave a sigh of relief.

'At last,' he said, grinning at George and stood aside with a bow to let Faro precede him into the carriage. Lacking the extravagant furnishings of the Orient Express it was nevertheless comfortable, a blissful haven after their recent ordeal.

'Isn't it wonderful?' said George bouncing up and down on the plush chairs.

The railway official, consulting an important-looking gold watch on a handsome gold chain, assured his royal passenger that they should reach the border in less than forty minutes. The watch snapped shut, the signal was given to the waiting guard and after some strains, jerkings and renewed steam they were off at a steady pace down the line.

'Soon we'll be home. Just think,' said George, 'won't it be wonderful, Anton? All our familiar things again, there waiting for us.'

Staring out of the window the two boys lapsed into German as they talked excitedly of horses, and games and the archery field.

Suddenly aware of Faro again, Anton smiled. 'Tell him, George, you are better than the English Robin Hood.'

George shook his head. 'He is exaggerating.'

'No, I am not. I've seen you.' And to Faro. 'Archery is our national sport.'

'In the Middle Ages,' George said, 'Luxorian archers were famous and fought as mercenaries with many European armies. They went on the Crusades too.'

'The President prefers guns and soldiers,' said Anton grimly.

At this reminder of what might lie ahead, Faro wished he could share the boys' excitement and confidence in the future. It seemed absurd that he could not shake off the growing certainty of danger still to come.

He found himself staring out of the window anxiously scrutinising the horizons for any signs of movement. That twitch of unease remained that they had not yet seen the last of this bleak and threatening landscape.

His two young travelling companions had no such misgivings. With all the resilience of youth they had recovered from their recent ordeals and begged to be allowed to ride on the engine.

The guard was summoned to escort them and Faro was delighted to enjoy a little peace and quiet in the very comfortable carriage. Though not as elegant as the Orient Express, it had attractive features and a very distinctive style. The wooden panels were hand-painted with highly decorated scenes that he associated with travel in Europe. Swiss-style houses and mountain peaks covered in snow, with edelweiss predominant on their sunny slopes.

He was delighted to lean back in a comfortable chair unobtrusively anchored to the floor by the window, and a few moments later the carriage door opened to admit a splendidly uniformed waiter with a food-laden tray. Fresh coffee, warm croissants, ham and cheese. A selection of good things for any man's breakfast, especially one as hungry as Faro at that moment.

The young gentlemen, he was told, had elected to have food brought to them on the engine. They did not wish to miss any of the journey.

Faro was surprised to realise he understood every word. The waiter smiled. Then Faro remembered that English was the second language of Luxoria and that even minor officials would be well-versed in the language.

He watched the passing landscape as he ate. Although there was still little colour, there was less snow than he had expected and a marked improvement had taken place in the terrain. Meadows, vast orchards, with deciduous forests on the hillsides' lower slopes, changing into conifers as the trees ascended. Vineyards and glimpses of twisting rivers and water mills. Here and there the turret of a castle frowned down from within a deep forest. There was an odd familiarity about the scenery. He had a sense of *déjà vu.*

Suddenly he knew why. This area reminded him of Royal Deeside. He laughed out loud. No wonder Prince Albert had chosen Balmoral and been so very much at home there. When His Royal Highness felt wistful, by narrowing his eyes and imagining those tall Scottish pine forests above the River Dee replaced with vineyards and a twisting river from his homeland, he could have been in Saxe-Coburg again.

'We will be arriving at the border in a short while, sir. We should be inside Luxoria within the hour,' the waiter told him, coming to collect his tray and take any further orders.

The head of the State Railway appeared, bowed and announced, 'We are still in Germany at present, sir. We were given special permission to cross over on this minor branch line, now closed except for freight trains, to collect our very important royal passenger.'

To Faro's enquiry regarding sending a telegraph to Heidelberg, he was assured that there were always such facilities available at the border post.

So he relaxed in his comfortable chair for a while longer, viewing the landscape as it flashed by, a constant source of interest. He must remember any particular details that Imogen would want to know about.

It would be such a delight to be with her again, he thought, forcing her image to the front of his mind to obliterate the sadness of the inevitable parting from George. He was aware that there was not the remotest possibility of ever seeing his son again, of watching the boy become a man and eventually the ruler of Luxoria.

He sighed. He must guard against over-indulgence in sentiment, remembering always with gratitude that he had shared a few precious days of the boy's existence and had been instrumental in returning him safely to his mother. As for himself, he would be the practical traveller once again, taking an ordinary service train back to Stuttgart. A telegraph to Imogen would have her meeting him in Heidelberg.

He smiled at the thought of how surprised she would be and of the great adventure he had to relate to her. Was the time now ripe to tell her the truth about George?

How would she react? –

The sound of the train rhythmically chug-chugging along was very hypnotic. He would rest his eyes just for a moment.

Perhaps he slept. Suddenly he was aware that he was no longer alone. Confused, he opened his eyes, to find Dieter looking down at him.

22

'Dieter!'

The man smiled. 'Mr. Faro, I am sorry to disturb you. You were looking very peaceful. I am very glad indeed to see you safe and well. And the two boys – I am sorry I was not here to welcome you.'

Faro stared at him. 'When did you board the train?'

'Some time ago, Mr Faro. You must excuse me but like yourselves I was very tired by all my travels.' He sighed deeply. 'After giving orders that the boys and yourself were to be well looked-after, I said I did not wish to be disturbed until we were in sight of Luxoria.'

With a thin-lipped smile he added, 'They took me at my word. I fell asleep and I am afraid you came aboard unobserved.'

Faro listened to him, not believing a word of it. He remembered the boys shouting, the welcome. 'You must be a very heavy sleeper,' he said.

'Oh I am, very,' Dieter said smoothly. 'I had little chance of rest after I left you. I had to make my way to the telegraph office and –

it was very trying – I found it was closed until morning. I had to wait all night and then there were many complications that I will not bore you with.'

'I take it that you were not attacked by brigands? We feared that you had been taken prisoner by them.'

'Brigands!' Dieter gave a start of surprise. 'You saw brigands at the railway hut?'

'We did indeed, and Anton was taken hostage.'

'Anton!' His eyelids fluttered briefly and again Faro suspected that his surprise was feigned. 'I gather that since I am told both boys are enjoying the ride on the engine at this moment, Anton took no ill from his experience.'

'He managed to escape. Apparently they did not make him prisoner and, in fact, he thought he recognised them as some of the President's guards.'

Dieter shook his head, a somewhat unconvincing gesture. 'That is a very odd happening. Why should the President have Anton taken prisoner?'

'Why indeed? His own son,' said Faro drily.

That broke through Dieter's calm. 'Er, Anton told you that?'

'George did.'

Dieter shook his head and said gravely, 'It was to be kept a secret, Mr Faro, for obvious reasons. Anton is illegitimate but his father is fond of him and wished him to accompany his own son to Scotland. You realise it would have been very degrading both to the President and to Anton for his fellow-pupils to know his true background.' He shook his head and continued. 'Especially knowing how the other boys would react to such information. They would have made his life unbearable.'

'Do you know what happened at the railway hut to George and myself and the porter?'

'No.' Dieter frowned. 'I presume, like myself, you made your way to the telegraph office.'

'We were doing so when the hut was blown up.'

Dieter blinked as if in disbelief. 'Blown up! How dreadful. Who would do such a thing?'

'The same soldiers who took Anton.'

'But why, Mr Faro? Why should they do that if it was Anton they wanted?'

'The explosion was planned deliberately. But first they were to make sure that Anton, their main concern, was safe.' With a pause to let that sink in, he went on: 'You are an intelligent man, Dieter, you know something, I am sure, of the devious workings of Luxorian politics. Surely it is obvious to you that whoever was in charge of this hostage-taking and destruction of the railway hut, George was the real target.'

'I cannot imagine such a thing, Mr Faro,' Dieter said coldly. 'And your reasoning is beyond me.'

'Then might I ask you to consider some more of my reasoning, as you call it. May we talk about Glenatholl for a moment?'

'Glenatholl?' Dieter frowned as if he had some difficulty in remembering the place. 'I do not follow you.'

'First of all, I would like to discuss the accident to George's bodyguard Tomas.'

Dieter shrugged impatiently. 'I have already told you that it was an unfortunate accident that could happen to anyone. He fell out of the window. I thought you knew that, Mr Faro. You were on the premises when it happened.'

Faro smiled grimly. 'You did not know then that Tomas came to see me just before I gave my lecture. He had some urgent secret information, concerning George.'

Dieter looked uneasy. 'And that was?' he demanded sharply.

'We will leave that for the moment,' Faro said smoothly. 'I should like you to tell me instead about Helga and why she pretended to be leaving us in Paris when I saw her on the train at Strasbourg.'

'Mr Faro,' said Dieter wearily. 'She did leave us at Paris.'

'What about that ball of knitting wool?'

Dieter held up a hand in protest. 'We have gone into all that, Mr Faro. I can only insist once again that you were mistaken. As I told you at the time, it could not have been Helga. She was ill and wished to stay with her grandmother.'

'Very well. Tell me, how well did you know Helga?'

Dieter spread his hands wide. 'Hardly at all. I hardly remember her from Glenatholl. She was a servant and I had little to do with the domestic staff. I had exceptional duties looking after Anton and George. I was not interested in Helga, if that is what you are asserting, Mr Faro, I simply accepted what she told me.'

'To return to Anton. He has confessed all about George's kidnapping.'

'Has he indeed?' Again that flicker of uncertainty in the man's expression. 'I presume he has told you that it was really his idea, a practical joke to play on George.'

'A curious practical joke. Like the one on the ferry. To pretend someone tried to throw him overboard.'

Dieter made no denial, just a weary shrug of indifference. 'The kidnapping was a wager from the boys in his class. Anton insisted that I must help him if it was to succeed.'

'That was not quite Anton's version,' Faro interrupted. Dieter looked startled. 'But do go on.'

'We were to leave George in the old stable overnight.'

'With no regard to the dangers to his health, lying bound on a cold floor for hours,' Faro, said indignantly.

Dieter laughed grimly. 'He is a very strong child. Well used to the rigours of sleeping out all night. One of Glenatholl's more spartan exercises is camping in the hills, survival in the open air with only one blanket. What I did not know when I agreed to what seemed a harmless schoolboy's prank was that Captain Reece and the royal train would be arriving that day to take George to Balmoral.'

'Did Anton know?'

'I am sure he did. George tells him everything.' Another weary sigh. 'Mr Faro, you are always searching for reasons. I put it to you that Anton had a very good one for pretending that George was kidnapped.'

'And that was?'

'Jealousy, Mr Faro, just plain jealousy. Surely that must have occurred to you, seeing them together. Anton was jealous of George being invited to a shooting party at the home of your Queen. Left out because he is his father's natural son, unacknowledged whereas his half-brother is the rightful heir to Luxoria. Anton's mother was a German actress while George's mother is the Grand Duchess Amelie, a relative of the late Prince Consort and goddaughter of the Queen of England.'

He paused. 'Surely you can see Anton's motives in all of this. And I would say, although I have no experience of children, it seems perfectly normal that now and again Anton wants to prove he is as good as George in every way. You have already mentioned another example of his passion for practical jokes, you saw it on the ferry going to Calais.'

'Were you involved in that too?' Faro asked.

'No. That was one he thought out all by himself. But he confessed later that it had just been to scare George.'

'Not quite the story he has told us, that it was your idea, to test my powers as a detective,' Faro said.

Again no denial came from Dieter, who was watching him carefully. 'Perhaps it is difficult for a foreigner – and a policeman from another country – to understand how things work where kingdoms are at stake.'

Pausing a moment, he said slowly, 'I do not think you have fully realised, Mr Faro, that Anton has a lot to gain, worth fighting for and telling a few lies for, if George should meet with a fatal accident. Bearing this in mind I would advise you not to trust him or listen to all he says. He pretends to be a good friend to George, but – ' he shrugged, 'Anton is a very good actor, he can be very convincing, even shedding tears.'

141

And Faro remembered that extraordinary emotional scene on the railway track and earlier his tearful Prince Arthur in the scenes from Shakespeare entertainment at Glenatholl.

Who was he to believe? The answer was taken from him by a sudden interuption as the door was flung open as the boys rushed in. They were as taken aback as Faro had been to see Dieter there quite unharmed. As he told them what had happened, the train began to slow down.

George ran to the window. 'Luxoria! Hurray, Anton, we are home!'

The train had stopped. The guard came in and before he said a word, Faro knew something was wrong.

23

'Why have we stopped?' Dieter demanded of the guard.

'There is a change of plan, sir.'

Brushing the guard aside, the head of the State Railway appeared. Bowing, he said, 'We regret the delay, but we have received an urgent message that the train is not to proceed until further notice.'

'What do you mean, not proceed?' demanded Dieter.

Another bow. 'The royal train is to remain here.'

'Remain? For what purpose?'

Not only Dieter looked angry, the two boys were very upset indeed. As for Faro, he felt only despair that his intuition had been right. It had all been too easy and his happy sigh of relief that his mission to Luxoria was over had been somewhat premature. The whiff of danger in the air was not only due to the steam rising from the stationary royal train.

'I am sure we will not have long to wait, sir,' said the official.

Faro looked out of the window. A small cloud of dust on the horizon revealed itself as a band of horsemen rapidly heading in the direction of the train.

At his side, Anton and George exchanged alarmed glances which Faro shared. Had the so-called brigands caught up with Anton for escaping and stealing one of their horses? Or was George their target? This time, surely, there would be no mistake.

Dieter looked over their shoulders and turned quickly to the railway official.

'I insist that the train proceeds through the border. At once. That is the President's command.'

The man shook his head. With considerable dignity he replied 'I regret to say, sir, that, as you are probably aware, our President's commands are not applicable while our locomotive is resting on German soil.' Drawing himself up, he saluted and added, 'These orders are direct from the Imperial Headquarters and it would create an international incident should I have the temerity to ignore them.'

'Damn your orders,' said Dieter through clenched teeth. 'Obey mine! I am in charge here! Perhaps this will persuade you to change your mind.' And taking a revolver from his pocket he flourished it in the face of the astonished and now terrified official.

Faro only got the gist of what was being said, but it was enough for him to seize Dieter's wrist. 'Why don't you wait and see what is happening out there? Surely a short delay won't make any difference.'

The troop of horsemen was nearer now. Faro sighed gratefully. Those black-and-silver uniforms could never have been mistaken for the red bandanas of Anton's so-called kidnappers.

'Get this train going! Immediately!' shouted Dieter, at the sight of the new arrivals, and Faro had to grasp the arm in which Dieter held his revolver as the reason for his anxiety became clearer.

Were the Hussars intending to kidnap the Luxorian train? Was that why he was so upset? Faro wondered, as he watched the leader of the troop leap on to the engine.

His footsteps came towards them. The door opened to reveal a colonel, splendid in black and silver and wearing a shako with the skull-and-crossbones emblem. It was the uniform of the Death's Head Hussars, Kaiser Wilhelm's crack regiment.

The boys ran towards the newcomer and yelled in unison, 'Uncle Karl!'

The Colonel roared with laughter, put an arm around both lads and sternly nodded towards Dieter, who was still holding the revolver he had been using to threaten the railway official.

Stretching out his hand, the Colonel said sternly, 'You will not be needing that any longer, since you are almost home. You are not in any danger.' He bowed. 'You may cross the border and proceed into Luxoria.'

Dieter took a deep breath. 'Excellent! Perhaps you would care to tell me what all this delay is about. Or is it just an idle moment for a family reunion?'

The Colonel ignored him and bowed towards Faro, clicking his heels. 'We have not been introduced,' and to George, 'Perhaps you will do the necessary.'

Beaming, George introduced Faro to his uncle, adding proudly, 'Mr Faro saved both our lives, Anton and me. We owe it all to him, Uncle Karl. Will you please see that he is properly rewarded?'

'Of course.' Another clicking of heels produced a weary sigh from Dieter.

'May we now proceed, Colonel? With your permission.'

The Colonel regarded him solemnly. 'You may proceed, by all means, sir.'

'Thank you.'

'I have not finished. I have said you may proceed into Luxoria, with the royal train.' He paused. 'Alone.' And cutting short Dieter's protest, he added, 'His Highness and Anton are to remain with me here in Germany.'

'What!' Dieter demanded angrily. 'I have my orders to deliver Anton personally to his father.'

The Colonel shook his head and Dieter shouted, 'You will answer for this. He is the President's son.'

The Colonel smiled. 'He comes with me by his mother's wishes, who still has legal custody of their son.' At Faro's puzzled expression, he explained. 'She is my sister, and Anton my nephew. Is that not so, Anton?' he asked gently.

'Yes, Uncle Karl. But I wish to stay with George,' he said moving closer to the boy he believed was his half-brother.

'Please, Uncle Karl,' George added.

Dieter could hardly conceal his fury. 'Very well. We will see what the President has to say about this. Meanwhile, I am to return George to his mother the Grand Duchess, who is eagerly awaiting his arrival in the royal palace.'

The Colonel shook his head. 'You have been misinformed. The Grand Duchess is still in Mosheim at the Kaiser's hunting-lodge where she has remained since her accident.'

Dieter looked even more angry. Touching his pocket, he said, 'I have here a telegraph saying that she is well and awaiting George.' He turned to the boy. 'You read it.'

It was George's turn to look bewildered. He shook his head. 'How do we know it was from her, Dieter? Anyone can send a telegraph message. Helga could have sent it when she left us in Paris.'

Faro gave him an admiring glance. The boy was sharp and the full measure of the plot to separate him from his mother was now beginning to emerge. The reason for Anton's so-called kidnapping to get him safe to the President. And when Gustav knew that George had survived the journey and the bomb attempt, Faro feared that his days would be numbered once he set foot in Luxoria.

'Are we ready to leave?' asked the Colonel. 'Very well, if you care to look out of the window, Anton, you will see that the Imperial train is approaching on the line behind us. We just transfer from one to the other.'

With their luggage gathered together, the boys and Faro jumped down on to the track. An angry-faced Dieter watched them from the window and the Colonel went over and spoke to him briefly as the train gathered up steam to cross the border into Luxoria. Not even Anton gave Dieter a backward glance or offered a word of thanks to his ex-bodyguard.

The Imperial train was waiting for them some hundred yards down the line. The carriages were painted dark blue and ivory outside, the Kaiser's drawing-room carriage, as Faro was soon to discover, was magnificent in upholstered blue silk with crystal chandeliers that tinkled like musical chimes as the train moved smoothly on its way.

Such delights were of no interest to George and Anton who insisted, with Uncle Karl's permission, that once again they ride on the engine, a much grander locomotive than the one they had just left, with engineers and footplatemen in tall hats and frock coats.

The Colonel relaxed in the chair opposite Faro. Removing his shako he took out a gold cigar case. Faro declined the offer. At that moment he would have given much for a pipe of tobacco and a dram – or several – of an excellent Scotch whisky.

He was intrigued by the magnificence of the Colonel – the uniform, the splendid moustache, the famous Prussian 'peg-top' haircut. The lightest brightest blue eyes now regarding him with equal curiosity and ready to crinkle into merriment could, he did not doubt, also turn to ice. Even on this, the merest acquaintance, Faro felt that beyond the bravura there lurked an honest man, one he would trust with his life. It was the same instinct that had made him dislike and distrust Dieter from the very outset of their journey.

After some polite exploratory conversation in which the Colonel continued to regard him with that friendly but curious intensity, it became clear that he had reached the same deadly conclusions about the President's actions regarding George's future.

'I presume that the fake telegraph regarding his mother, sent to the Orient Express, was arranged with one of the man's fellow-conspirators. Once the President had him back in Luxoria, he would be useful as a hostage.'

'A hostage?' asked Faro. 'I don't understand. It seems to me that he would want to get rid of him more permanently.'

'By no means, though that might have come later. First he planned to use George as an instrument to give the President enormous bargaining power over the Grand Duchess – and Luxoria. He knew that Amelie would give anything – anything – '

He paused and added what Faro already knew. 'It is my opinion that she would sign any agreement to save her only son. Even to handing over the country and forsaking all future rights of George as heir. That is how much the boy means to her.'

'And the Grand Duchess's health?' Faro put in carefully, trying not to sound too eager for the news he longed to hear.

'She is recovering. The spray of bullets which killed the two servants hit her near the right lung. Her life was despaired of, but with the Kaiser's excellent doctors, although she is still very weak, she has a good chance of survival.'

The Colonel paused. 'There is another matter of Luxorian politics which you might not be able to understand, another reason for George's bargaining power. It has long been well-known amongst those of us who are close to the Kaiser – myself included as a lifelong friend – that he wishes to annex Luxoria to Imperial Germany.'

'So I have heard,' said Faro. And when the Colonel's eyebrow raised a little at that, he added, 'We have our sources of secret information too.'

The Colonel laughed. 'Of course, a senior policeman in the service of Her Majesty Queen Victoria. Stupid of me!'

'I begin to see your reasoning, Colonel.'

'Excellent! Proceed.'

'The President could use George's future to force his mother to refuse the Kaiser's wish for annexation with Germany.'

The Colonel shook his head. 'I think you are oversimplifying matters a little, Mr Faro. George has no "future" as far as the President is concerned. He is expendable, since the President wishes to have his natural son Anton as heir to Luxoria.'

148

'But surely George is his legitimate heir.'

The Colonel smiled. 'Ah, now there is a point! Suppose we ask why Gustav should want to destroy George, the son of his marriage, forced perhaps but legal, to Amelie.'

Leaning forward, he raised a finger. 'The answer is very plain, surely – ' Pausing, he laughed, 'especially to a detective of your powers, Mr Faro.'

'I don't follow you,' said Faro, trying to look blank despite his fast beating heart.

The Colonel shook his head, and said triumphantly. 'George is not his child.'

They were interrupted by the arrival of a waiter bearing some excellent schnapps. Not quite Faro's preference but, at that moment, strong enough to down in one gulp and hopefully still the anguish of hearing what the Colonel had to impart.

'Permit me to let you into a secret, Mr Faro.'

24

Pausing, the Colonel looked out of the window. 'This secret goes back a long time and is a very personal one.'

Sighing, he smiled. 'I have been in love with Amelie for a very long time. But to go back to the beginning, Wilhelm – the Kaiser – and I were childhood companions. I knew all his secrets. He told me how he had met this wonderful lady while visiting his grandmother Queen Victoria at Balmoral.'

He paused. 'I believe you know it well, Mr Faro, and that you are a trusted intimate of Her Majesty.'

Faro bowed. 'Hardly that, sir. I have been a useful servant only, on many occasions.'

The Colonel laughed. 'Ah, like John Brown, perhaps. The servant who taught her to enjoy your Scotch whisky in her tea.'

And Faro smiled wryly at another reputation ruined by crossing the English Channel. 'No, sir. I am a policeman – a detective – I was on hand on several occasions when there were threats to her life.'

'Ah, yes – assassination attempts like the one on Amelie?'

Faro nodded. 'Very similar.'

'And you were able to avert them. A pity you had not been present at Mosheim.' Again that intense look. 'I understand that you were also responsible for Amelie's safety when she visited Scotland some years ago.'

'I was.'

The Colonel smiled. 'Scotland has a fascination for us, a beautiful country. I once had the honour to accompany Wilhelm. He loves his grandmother, a rather formidable lady, according to Bismarck.' Pausing, he asked, 'Did you ever meet His Imperial Majesty?'

'I never had that pleasure.'

'A pity, for he is a remarkable man. Not only as my good friend but as a statesman and a soldier. Someone once said of him that he is eager to impress everyone. That he wants to be the bride at every wedding and the corpse at every funeral. He is a great raconteur, few can match him telling a story. And physically too.'

His face darkened momentarily as he continued. 'He has over-come a physical disadvantage that is not publically referred to,' he touched his left arm delicately, 'to become a great horseman. You must be wondering why I am telling you, a stranger, all these things, Mr Faro. The reason is very obvious. Compare this man with what you know of Amelie's husband, President Gustav.'

He shrugged. 'The man is a savage, a moral degenerate. Would it surprise anyone that Amelie, a beautiful cultured woman, would prefer His Imperial Majesty to such a fellow?'

Faro listened, fascinated now. They had come some distance from George's parentage, but was the Colonel hinting that he thought that Wilhelm was the boy's father?

'We were all a little in love with the unhappy Grand Duchess that Wilhelm had brought into our small circle. We all wished to see her free of such a marriage. My own reasons were intensely personal. My sister Melissa was born with the gift of a voice, she defied family tradition by going on the stage. Gustav saw her, charmed her by some means unknown to the rest of us. Perhaps his savage background had a sexual fascination after her gentle upbringing.'

He stopped and sighed again. 'Who knows? She was young, beautiful, ambitious and with a passionate nature. She became his mistress and Anton was born. As his own marriage was childless after many years, he decided to be rid of Amelie, and marry my sister.'

He shook his head. 'For me this was a very difficult situation personally. I was in love with Amelie.' Smiling gently, he added, 'And I still am. I have been faithful to her for many years.'

Pausing again, he regarded Faro. 'I am telling you all this because there is a mystery which has long intrigued me and one I hope you might be able to solve. It is rather personal, but I gather from your dealings with Amelie's godmother, your Queen, that you are a man of discretion, a man who can be trusted with secrets.'

He looked at Faro as if expecting some affirmative and when there was none, he went on. 'As you know, Amelie went to Scotland all those years ago to seek refuge from Gustav. Her life was in constant danger. There had been attempts to poison her to clear the way for Melissa who, of course, would not listen to any of us. She adored Gustav and wanted to marry him, have their child legitimised and made his heir.'

With a shake of his head, he added bitterly: 'She has learned the truth about Gustav, but all too late. But that is another story. When Amelie returned to Luxoria, it was for a reconciliation with Gustav and I am afraid my foolish sister was distraught when this resulted in a child. Immediately her own relationship with Gustav began to fall apart. She had served her purpose and now she was no longer needed. There were other younger, prettier girls he could take as mistresses and she returned to her neglected career.'

'Had he any other children by these unions?' Faro asked.

The Colonel smiled. 'Your question interests me exceedingly,

Mr Faro. We are obviously thinking along the same lines. But he has no other offspring than Anton, that we are aware of.'

Pausing he looked out of the window. The landscape had changed, in Faro's eyes confirming the reason why the Prince Consort had found Deeside so attractive.

The Colonel said, 'We will soon be at the end of our journey and I must make haste since the two boys will be returning to the carriage and we may have no further chance of an intimate conversation like this. And I will go on never knowing the answer to this little mystery.'

'How do you think I can help you, sir?' asked Faro, knowing that four simple words could clear up the mystery of George's birth, four simple words that would never pass his lips.

The Colonel put his fingertips together and regarded Faro gravely. 'In your short acquaintance with Amelie, was there anyone in Scotland with whom she might have had a temporary infatuation?'

Regardless of his fast-beating heart, Faro said: 'I cannot answer that. We met only briefly during a visit to her friends in East Lothian, near Edinburgh.'

'Then there might have been someone at this place?' the Colonel asked eagerly.

Shaking his head, Faro said truthfully, 'I hardly think that would be possible. There were no suitable or eligible men from my acquaintance with that family.'

The Colonel looked disappointed and, frowning over his schnapps, Faro felt uncomfortably aware of his penetrating gaze. At last he shrugged.

'Perhaps I am all wrong, what you call "barking up the wrong tree".'

Faro pretended to be puzzled. 'You have said yourself that there was a reconciliation, so why shouldn't George be the President's child?'

'Because, Mr Faro, Gustav has found out the truth.'

'I don't understand,' lied Faro, who understood perfectly.

The Colonel spread his hands wide. 'All the evidence is confirmed by things that have happened lately. The assassination attempt at Mosheim – who else would want to be rid of Amelie, who else realises that this annexation with Imperial Germany would topple the President from his power?'

Faro's thoughtful expression suggested that he was considering this possibility. 'But if this is such a well-kept secret, about the child, how could he have found out?'

The Colonel shrugged. 'Who knows? In a moment of terror or desperation, perhaps Amelie confessed the truth. Certainly his behaviour towards George – Amelie is terrified of what might happen to the boy – seems to confirm that the President is now aware that the boy is not his son.'

Pausing to let this sink in, he added, 'I have known and loved Amelie for a long time. I have asked her to marry me, knowing it was unlikely although my blood is better than that of her President. In Germany the Junkers are country gentry, a noble class of landowners formed in the Middle Ages. They do not correspond to any other society in Europe. We belong to men who are not too proud to join their estate workers during the harvest but are proud of their right to carry a sword for the King of Prussia.'

He smiled. 'So I have always loved Amelie, always hoped that she perhaps loved me a little. But one day, when she was staying at Mosheim, she told me that although she was grateful she could never return my affection. And she hinted – just a mere hint – that there was someone else. Someone she had loved from the first day she met him and would love to the very last day of her life.'

He shook his head, as though still bewildered. 'It was a great shock to me. I had never suspected such a thing.'

'Perhaps the Kaiser?' said Faro helpfully, just to ease the tension.

'No. I am sure of that. We have talked of Amelie's little mystery, Wilhelm and I. He is somewhat vague and at one time I suspected they might have been lovers, very briefly.'

'You might be right,' was the cautious response.

'No,' said the Colonel emphatically. Leaning forward he subjected Faro once again to that intense gaze. 'The secret lies in your country. Someone she met, someone we know nothing about, a brief love for a mysterious man her heart still aches for. Whoever he was, that man is undoubtedly also George's father.'

The train was beginning to slow down. The Colonel sat back and gave him a brilliant smile. 'We are almost at our destination. Come along, Mr Faro. We have only minutes for you to solve my mystery. Surely, before we part, Scotland's greatest detective must have some clue to offer about the man's identity.'

25

Faro was spared any further interrogation regarding George's parentage as the train slowed down.

'Ah, we are there!' said the Colonel.

Faro looked out of the window. The terrain with its pine forests and undulating hills and river did not immediately suggest the outskirts of a great city.

'Stuttgart?' he said.

The Colonel laughed. 'No. But this is where we leave for Mosheim. Unfortunately a railway line does not yet exist but it will in time. It is on the list of the Kaiser's projects but he has been persuaded against it by the Kaiserin since once royal associations make Mosheim popular with the masses, their privacy will be destroyed.'

Faro wondered how he could politely take his leave of the Colonel and insist on continuing on the train to Stuttgart. The Colonel had observed his bleak expression and realised that he did not look very enthusiastic at this change of plans. 'You do not wish to accompany us?'

Faro smiled. 'I was hoping to take a train to Heidelberg. I am meeting a friend there.'

'A lady, perhaps?' The Colonel gave him a teasing glance. 'A romantic meeting?'

Faro's enigmatic smile was rightly interpreted.

'Can this impatient lady wait a little longer? I believe the Grand Duchess is very anxious to see you, to thank you personally for bringing George to her.'

This piece of news made Faro groan inwardly. Meeting Amelie again, with George at his side, was something he had hoped to avoid.

'It is inconvenient, yes?' asked the Colonel anxiously.

'A little.'

'But we will only delay your journey by a few days,' he insisted. 'And Mosheim is a place you should see. It dates back to Roman times, indeed the remains of a Roman settlement have been found here. Once it was a monastic town.'

But Faro wasn't listening any more. How could he find a valid excuse to decline Amelie's invitation? Did she know he was coming? Would she be equally embarrassed? What would it be like for those closest to her to meet him?

He cursed the resemblance between himself and George, evident to even a casual observer. Anyone seeing them together must guess the truth. Remembering the shock of seeing their reflections he wondered whether others were as observant. He was certain that Dieter had guessed, or was that the workings of his guilty conscience?

'I had hoped to send a telegraph to my friend from Stuttgart,' he told the Colonel, who laughed.

'If that is all, Mr Faro, I can assure you it will be taken care of. We have excellent facilities on board the train. The Kaiser has thought of everything for his passengers' and his own comfort.'

Pausing, he added, 'I wish you to stay also. I have enjoyed our short acquaintance. And I am secretly hoping that a meeting with

Amelie will jolt your memory regarding her visit to your country and the people she met. Perhaps it might provide some clues to the mystery concerning George.

'I also hope that you will have a chance to call upon my sister Melissa when you are in Heidelberg. She will want to meet the good man who looked after her son so well on the journey from Scotland.

'I have to make arrangements for his future, since he is unlikely to return to the Scottish college. I think perhaps the military academy but Melissa would rather he chose a less warlike career. He is like her and wishes to be an actor, which seems a very strange choice for a male from an old Junker family.'

Faro smiled. 'I can assure you he would do very well. He has a natural ability, from what I observed in the Shakespearean scenes put on by his school.' He explained that he had been a guest at the school on that occasion.

'Is that so? Then your judgement is indeed a recommendation to bear in mind, Mr Faro. The boy is young enough and with his mother's career, which is doing so well at present. she must leave his education in my hands as his legal guardian. I have little to do with children, I am afraid.'

Faro pushed to the back of his mind the darker side of Anton's acting ability that Dieter had stressed. The ability to shed tears at will, the screen for telling outrageous and convincing lies.

At that moment, the door opened to admit George and Anton. As George rushed over and sat down at his side, Faro felt again the intensity of the Colonel's disconcerting gaze.

Fortunately the two boys were full of questions. George was telling his uncle that he was longing to see his pet falcon again. There was a small menagerie at Mosheim, Faro gathered, kept for the Kaiser's shooting guests.

Steps were provided for the party to leave the train and in the small station precinct a carriage awaited to take them through the town and on to the Kaiserhof.

The Colonel pointed to a hillside with a dark forest. 'That is our destination, Mr Faro. It was once upon a time a Franciscan monastery, quite secluded. You will see it in due course.'

The drive through the town was picturesque enough for anyone's taste, thought Faro. There was a fairy-tale look about the ancient half-timbered houses leaning towards each other across narrow cobbled streets and the wide market-place dominated by an equestrian statue of some early benefactor staring reverently towards a handsome and equally ancient church, unmistakably a one-time fortification. The atmosphere of Mosheim recalled illustrations from the children's stories of the Brothers Grimm. Here was a place where anything could happen, wildly romantic and remote as a distant planet from stern-faced Scottish streets where tight-windowed grey houses paid careful tribute to respectability.

The passage of the royal carriage was enhanced by the ringing of church bells. They were not to greet young George of Luxoria however but to call people to mass.

Leaving the town behind, the horses began their strenuous upward climb on the last stage of the journey, along roads twisting up through the forest. Looking down, Faro saw a water-mill and a twist of river far below the treeline, the houses and church now reduced to the dimensions of a child's toy village.

Suddenly the forest cleared a little to reveal glimpses of a small castle, romantic and quite unreal.

So this was the hunting-lodge, the old castle Wilhelm's parents had discovered and renovated long ago in an area allegedly teeming with wildlife. Faro hadn't seen any. They remained prudently invisible, shy creatures like deer and fierce ones like wild boar.

The Kaiser had invested in strong gates for privacy and behind them a drive swept towards the front of the house. The boys leaped out of the carriage and dashed up the steps to the front door.

It seemed that there were other visitors present since a small army of carriages lined the drive. Faro, not looking forward to the unavoidable encounter with Amelie, was thankful that with others present, this would be a formal occasion.

The two boys had already disappeared inside the lodge and a waiting footman ushered the newcomers into a waiting-room, through a hall with walls overburdened with trophies of the hunt.

Deer, wild boar and eagles in glass cases stared down on them. Stepping cautiously across a fierce-headed tiger-skin rug, Faro felt depressed by the presence of so many dead things.

Watching his expression with some amusement, the Colonel said, 'Wilhelm tells us that your Balmoral is like this.'

'It is indeed,' said Faro and left it at that.

An equerry arrived, bowed and greeted the new arrivals. 'Her Highness is resting at present. She has been told of your arrival and will receive you shortly.'

The Colonel indicated chairs and ordered schnapps. As they sat by the sunny window Faro was not kept long in doubt of the identity of those other important visitors, who were just leaving.

'Count von Bismarck,' said the Colonel.

And Faro caught a glimpse of the legendary man of German politics, immensely tall and imposing as he came down the steps. Noticing the Colonel at the window, he saluted him gravely and, stepping into the leading carriage, drove off, followed by his retinue.

The Colonel sighed. 'A pity we didn't arrive earlier. I am sure he would have enjoyed a meeting with you. He is also a friend of Amelie, I expect he has business with her regarding Luxoria. Honest Otto they call him, since he has acted as broker between the European powers. He has built up a web of alliances and even enjoys a good press in your native land. When he met your Queen Victoria, he was very impressed. Told everyone: "What a woman! There is someone I could have dealings with".

'Twenty years ago, he made it his business to win over the German princes and created a unified Germany with Berlin as the capital. The Reich has become Europe's largest state, dominated by

Prussia. And it is always growing. Bismarck is a Junker like myself and that helped him achieve greatness, so some say.'

With a deep sigh he added, 'Alas, poor Bismarck.'

'Why do you say that? He doesn't sound like a man who needs anyone's pity.'

'Not on the surface, but I know a thing or two. Wilhelm isn't happy about him. They do not see eye to eye, Mr Faro. Bismarck is a politician of the old school, anti-socialist. Wilhelm has more modern ideas of extending our social security system. I am afraid when it comes to open warfare between the two, Bismarck may have to go. He will accept the inevitable with great dignity and Wilhelm will make it all very polite. That it is time for him to take honourable retirement.'

The door opened. A woman appeared, leaning on her servant's arm; a woman with regal presence, tall and slender, quite lovely, Faro thought, but with the fragility of crystal.

Her eyes sought him out, smiling.

He went forward and, bowing, realised that his image of her all these years had changed. It was like an out of focus painting, the colours of which had been disturbed, their margins blurred.

He looked up, confused.

She smiled at him. Her eyes were undeniably all that remained of his memory of the Grand Duchess Amelie.

'Welcome to Mosheim, Inspector Faro,' she said and held out her hand.

26

Amelie was used to hiding her emotions. That intimate glance of recognition and adoration faded swiftly and formality took its place.

George ran to her side, led her to a sofa and sat with his arm around her. They talked together for a few moments, laughed and kissed while the Colonel answered Anton's numerous questions about sport and shooting and pet animals. Faro suddenly found himself in the midst of a family circle from which he was excluded by more than his inability to follow the voluble German of this reunion.

Glad to retreat to the window and look down on the track through the forest towards the distant town, he knew he had served his purpose, his mission fulfilled. George was safe home again and he longed to be released, to breathe freely with no more anxieties in his life than catching the next train to Heidelberg.

Watching the little group, he was relieved that meeting Amelie again had touched no chord of lost love. His brief role in her life had been over long ago, played out almost before it began.

Was Amelie experiencing the same feelings of relief, ignoring him completely, involved only in the joy of having her son at her side again? Aware of his isolation, the Colonel approached.

'Perhaps you would care to retire for a while, Mr Faro. A room has been prepared for you.'

Faro shook his head. 'That is most kind, but I will not be needing it. I intend to leave shortly if you will provide me with a carriage to the railway station.'

The Colonel smiled. 'We cannot permit you to leave us so soon, Mr Faro.' And watching Faro's expression, he said, 'You must be our guest until tomorrow. My sister is arriving with a friend and you may perhaps travel back direct to Heidelberg in their carriage.'

He beamed. 'Will that not please you, no more trains for a while, Mr Faro? Besides, we wish to have your company for a little longer. We do not wish to lose such a good friend and one deserving a well-earned rest after his travels.'

Smiling, the Colonel regarded him. 'A room and a bath at your disposal – surely that is tempting. And a suit of clothes,' he added tactfully. At that Faro became aware with some embarrassment of his dishevelled appearance, which had not perturbed him in the least until then.

'There are always clothes in readiness for guests. Shooting parties are liable to be rained on, or have guests fall into muddy rivers,' the Colonel smiled.

At least he did not mention being subject to assassins, Faro thought, rubbing his chin and conscious that he badly needed a shave. A bath and a change of clothes would be welcome before meeting Imogen again, he decided, thanking the Colonel for his thoughtfulness.

The Colonel bowed. 'You are most welcome. It is a pity you will not have a chance to meet the Kaiser, he is absent at this time on a visit to Potsdam. He will be sorry to have missed you, since you are a devoted and trusted servant of his grandmother.'

How they liked to dwell on that, Faro thought as he was ushered

163

through the hall with its hunting trophies, stags and wild boar, whose fierce gaze relentlessly followed his progress up the staircase.

Inside the room they were replaced by walls hung with gilt-framed hunting scenes. Two of Mr Landseer's paintings of dead animals and birds suggested that they had originated from Balmoral, fond birthday gifts from devoted grandmother to favourite grandson.

As he closed the door, Faro once again found it depressing to be surrounded by so much dead and dying. The room was warmed by a closed stove and the huge canopied bed was at least inviting. On it, in readiness for his use, lay clothes and fresh linen. Handsome grey breeches and a jacket trimmed with hunting-green, complete with sportsman's hat, the uniform of the hunting-guest, he thought, appreciating an entire wardrobe of accessories.

He was delighted to find a full tub in the dressing-room, steaming warmly and ready for his use. Thankfully stripping off, he sank into it gratefully and decided that this was luxury indeed, peace and quiet and a hot bath. He closed his eyes.

He awoke with a start to find that beyond the window the sky had darkened. It was now late afternoon. Seizing the voluminous bathrobe he went back into the bedroom. A footman appeared, followed by a valet with razor and soap, a business-like towel over his arm.

Invited to sit in a chair, Faro enjoyed one of the few occasions his life had offered the luxury of what was in middle-class Edinburgh a pleasant daily visit from the barber. However, when a week's growth of beard was removed he felt suddenly naked and vulnerable.

It had also removed his last hope of disguise, his likeness to George was there for all the world to see.

He smiled sadly at his reflection as he dressed. A likeness most fathers would have been proud of, but for him a cruel twist of fate, and potentially fatal for himself and others.

Trying to thrust aside such gloomy thoughts, at last attired in his borrowed suit – which fitted very well, apart from being a trifle too short in the sleeves and a trifle too wide in the breeches – he was considering whether or not to wear the hat with its ridiculous feather when a tap on the door announced the Colonel.

'Ah! The new suit indeed becomes you, Mr Faro.' But Faro felt his gaze was more concerned with his now smooth and beardless countenance. If the truth came out on this visit, would the Colonel once again come to his aid?

'Amelie sends greetings. She will dine alone with George this evening.'

That was a relief, Faro thought.

'She is still very frail, you know,' the Colonel continued. 'Wilhelm's physicians have done their best for her, but she may always remain something of an invalid. Our other visitors are expected shortly. My sister and a friend from Heidelberg, as I mentioned to you. It may surprise you to know that Amelie and Melissa have formed a deep friendship, united by the cruel treatment of Gustav. At one time Melissa hated her, it was not reciprocated since if truth were told, and it seldom is, Amelie was relieved when her husband took a mistress. All that is past now, Anton and George and their respective mothers are firm friends, united by misfortune.

'Now you must excuse me as I have matters to attend to in Mosheim. Tedious, but there it is. I must apologise for leaving you to dine alone, but you will be well taken care of, I can assure you of that. Perhaps you would care to dine in your room here?'

Faro considered that prospect very agreeable. The thought of being waited upon by an army of servants alone at the huge dining table he had glimpsed across the hall, surrounded on all sides by the reproachful gaze of dead animals, had little appeal. And he recognised, not for the first time, the need for solitude, time to sort out all that had happened since he had left Edinburgh.

Silent-footed servants arrived. The lamps were lit, the stove replenished and it was with a feeling of great comfort that he sat down to the huge platter of food set before him. Roasted meat and vegetables, wine and rich dessert of chocolate and cream. Delicious! But he was to pay a price for this over-indulgence. His stomach, used to spartan fare, and little of it in the last few days, rebelled. He went to bed, fell asleep and awoke in such agony he was sure he had been poisoned.

His mind raced ahead. That was it! He had been invited to dine alone and someone had taken the opportunity of putting poison in the wine. Someone in President Gustav's pay.

Then common sense took over. He realised these symptons were those that had haunted him all his working life. Bad eating habits, acquired in long days with the Edinburgh City Police, had resulted in a digestive system which was one of Vince's cautionary tales. Would that he had Vince at hand instead of merely the packet of digestive powders in his valise.

He took one and decided dismally that it was useless and his suspicions had been right. A second dose and he began to feel relief as he lay back on his pillows thinking of the mad imaginings a simple attack of indigestion could bring.

Poison indeed!

But although he told himself he was being foolish, he was haunted by uneasy dreams and awoke next morning feeling slightly under the weather, with an inability to rid himself of that spine-tingling awareness of danger which had little to do with his faulty digestive system.

But who would want to harm him here, of all places? Looking out of his window at the front of the hunting-lodge, he realised this was the very place where the assassin had struck; where two of Amelie's servants had been slain and she herself almost fatally wounded.

Breakfast was brought to him. Coffee, warm bread, butter, ham and cheese. But he ate little.

He went downstairs, his feet echoing on the boards. The lodge seemed uneasily deserted and he almost jumped when a door opened to admit the Colonel.

After the usual polite questions about whether he had slept well, to which Faro gave polite but untruthful answers, he was told there was a message from Amelie.

'She wishes to show the kind policeman who did so much for her in Scotland one of her favourite places here in the Odenwald – once an old woodcutter's cottage that the Kaiser had restored and gave to her as a gift long ago. It has been a retreat for George and herself. She has already left with the two boys.

'There is a horse for you, ready saddled. The track is well-marked – I will direct you. It is less than a quarter kilometre away.'

Faro was in a quandary. Naturally the Colonel presumed that all men of any substance rode, knowing little of the circumstances of Edinburgh policemen. And Faro hated to confess that he had had little opportunity for equestrian pursuits since his boyhood days in Orkney as he followed the Colonel to the stables.

A horse was led out to a mounting block.

'He belongs to Anton. A gentle beast, well-behaved,' said the Colonel, patting the animal's neck. 'Thoroughly reliable,' he added as if aware of Faro's apprehensions.

Mounting was easier than he expected after so many years, and Faro moved off, watched anxiously by the Colonel. Trying to appear like an experienced horseman, he realised that with the Colonel's usual tact, a boy's horse had been selected for an indifferent rider.

As he proceeded up the track, taking his time, trotting slowly and carefully, a shot rang out. It was close by and Faro had a confused thought that there must be a shooting party, perhaps some of the servants bringing down game for the larder.

Another shot, closer at hand. The beast neighed, terrified, as Faro felt the wind of a bullet close to the horse's mane. It had narrowly missed him but was enough for the beast to rear.

Faro was unseated, lost his reins and fell to the ground. Stunned and winded by the fall, some instinct told him not to move. Whoever fired that shot, he was the target.

As he lay inert, as if he had been hit, he tried to decide on the next move.

Suddenly everything was becoming sickeningly clear to him. Perhaps this whole trip to Mosheim had been arranged. A trap for him, now that the truth about George's parentage was out. And with such a deadly secret and its political consequences, he was never to be allowed to leave alive.

Cautious footsteps were approaching. He was lying curled up, vulnerable, on the ground.

The terrified horse had vanished back down the track and Faro knew that death was very near. He was totally unarmed. His only hope lay in his killer believing he was dead.

He saw a pair of boots, well polished. The butt of a rifle. A kick at his ribs. A grunt of approval.

As long as his killer believed he was dead. If he could spring into action before the man had a chance to raise that rifle and fire again.

This time there would be no possibility of missing.

At point-blank range.

The man leaned over him, breathing heavily . . .

27

Like a coiled spring, Faro unwound, seized the man's legs and
threw him to the ground.

Dieter!

Taken by surprise, Dieter lost his grip on the rifle, which began
to roll away down the slope. Faro strove to hold his attacker and at
the same time reach the rifle, but Dieter was younger and stronger
and Faro realised that he was no match for him. A sudden blow in
his stomach had Faro retching, falling away, rolling, his gathering
momentum halted by a boulder which cannoned into his side.

He felt the agonising crack and the next moment, Dieter was
standing over him, the rifle pointed at his head.

'Mr Faro, you never learn, do you? Yes, I am going to kill you,
make no mistake about that this time. I have my orders.'

'I thought you went back on the train to Luxoria,' gasped Faro,
fighting for breath and playing for time.

'I jumped off and made my way here – and here I am. This is our
last meeting, you shall die here, and I shall have carried out my part
in the the plan.'

'What plan?'

'Mr Faro, it was never intended that you should leave here alive. Especially when the truth was known.'

'What truth? I don't understand.'

Dieter gave him a thin-lipped smile. 'Everyone who has seen you with George must have guessed the truth. There are many disguises a man can have successfully, but when his offspring is his image – the President guessed some time ago that George was not his child. And now I think everyone who has seen you together knows. You are not a fool, Mr Faro, you must see that you have walked into a trap. You are a marked man, too dangerous to remain alive and I have orders to kill you.'

Faro sat up, each breath an agony.

'You can get to your feet if you wish. That will not help you. But you may choose how to die. There on the ground like a dog, or like an Englishman, bravely facing the firing squad,' Dieter added mockingly, clearly enjoying the situation.

'Thank you for your consideration,' said Faro, rising to his feet unsteadily, incapable of making any sudden moves, and without any hope of taking Dieter by surprise again.

Faint and dizzy with pain, certain that his ribs were cracked, his shoulder agonising, perhaps broken, he leaned weakly against a tree for support. He knew that there was no escape, only a few minutes remained of a life that was almost over.

What a way to go, he thought bitterly. That he of all people, with all his experience, should have walked into such a trap! There was no comfort in knowing that this trap was one no father could have resisted when the bait was his own son.

Dieter seemed in no hurry to kill him. Was his leisurely manner regret? Faro did not think so. More likely a sadistic enjoyment of having his victim helpless before him.

Occasionally he glanced beyond Faro down the track, his face expressionless. Who was he expecting?

Whoever it was Dieter did not seem perturbed or anxious and

Faro realised he need not entertain hopes of a last-minute rescue party. Tempting fate, he said, 'Well, I am ready. Get it over with. What are you waiting for?'

Dieter smiled grimly, shrugged. 'I am in no hurry. You have been very clever, Mr Faro – indeed there were times I almost began to like you. To feel that we had much in common, the paid policeman and the paid bodyguard.'

'Or the paid assassin,' Faro put in sourly. But curiously he had sometimes felt aware of their similarities. Could it be that Dieter had finer feelings that might be appealed to? Even at this moment, could he be persuaded to let his helpless victim live?

'What happened to Helga?' Faro asked. 'Did you kill her?'

Dieter laughed. 'Helga! It was Helga you have to thank for realising immediately that you were George's father. She saw the likeness – a woman's intuition, of course.'

'You did not kill her for that.'

'I did not kill her at all. As far as I know she is in Germany with her family.'

'But you needed someone to send the telegraph to persuade George that his mother was in Luxoria.'

'Correct, Mr Faro. You have hit the nail on the head, as they say in your country. And I was speaking the truth when I told you she had never boarded the train with us,' he added reproachfully.

'And talking of trains,' Faro put in. Even now certain that he was to die within the next few moments, he felt impelled to know the truth.

'When you disappeared from the railway hut to risk wolves and worse to go to the telegraph office, I presume that was all part of the plan.'

Dieter smiled. 'I knew that the President's crack regiment was somewhere in the vicinity in readiness for the arrival of the Luxorian train. I thought of an excellent way of obeying orders that would greatly please the President for it was most economical. First they must kidnap Anton so that he would be safe.'

'And plant the explosives for the rest of us, was that it?' said Faro grimly.

Dieter nodded. 'Exactly. A time-saving measure.'

'To kill an innocent child?'

Dieter's expression did not change. 'Alas, the innocent often die with the guilty – such matters are not for me to decide, indeed they make little difference in my profession, one way or another, Mr Faro.'

He shrugged. 'George will die sooner or later, the President will see to that. And you have always been expendable.'

The man's cold-blooded dedication appalled Faro. What hope was there of mercy from such a man.

Suddenly there were sounds. A rider approaching fast up the steep track.

A rescuer after all, Faro thought hopefully. Until he saw relief on Dieter's face. And realised that this was the moment he had been waiting for.

Still covering Faro with the rifle, he motioned him into the open. Looking over his shoulder, Faro saw the Colonel dismounting and shouted,

'Thank God you arrived in time.'

But the Colonel ignored him and turning to Dieter, said in German, 'I heard a rifle shot. I thought it was all over.'

Even as Faro thought he had misinterpreted the fatal words, Dieter bowed. 'Mr Faro eluded that one. I thought you might want to deliver the *coup de grâce* personally.'

The Colonel shook his head and Faro stared at him unbelievingly. So he, too, was part of the plan.

Dieter shrugged. 'No? Very well.' And raising the rifle. 'Farewell, Mr Faro.'

And Faro closed his eyes. Goodbye, George. Goodbye, world.

He heard the explosion. But he was still alive.

Dieter was lying on the ground. Dead with a bullet through his forehead.

Birds were screaming overhead and there were other sounds, faint voices echoing far-off.

The pistol in the Colonel's hand was turned towards him.

Suddenly the sky fell in on him and the darkness of death once more enfolded him.

28

He was being torn apart by wild animals, one of them was ripping off his shoulder.

Faro screamed and opened his eyes to find he was propped up on a bed in the hunting-lodge. An elderly man, presumably a doctor, was bending over him, tying a bandage across his chest. Behind him stood Colonel Karl zu Echlenberg, the man he had trusted. The man who had ordered his execution.

The doctor spoke a few words to the Colonel, bowed and left them.

'Your ribs are broken but our good doctor has set your dislocated shoulder. The pain of it made you pass out. It was as well you were unconscious when we carried you back. Very painful – I am sorry about that.'

'It could have been worse,' was Faro's laconic reply.

The Colonel sat down by the bedside, shook his head and said, 'I could not let him kill you. Even had I wished to do so, it was too late,' he added wryly, 'since George and Anton had appeared on the scene. They had been on the archery course, heard the shots – '

'Then it was true – what Dieter told me.'

The Colonel nodded. 'That you were never meant to leave Luxoria alive. To bring George back and then you were to be disposed of.'

'What was it to be? What had you in mind?' Faro asked bitterly.

He smiled grimly. 'A convenient accident, Mr Faro. This is just one of the sad facts of political necessity. You are not a foolish man, surely you can realise that.'

'Did Amelie know?' Faro put in anxiously.

'Of course not,' was the scornful reply. 'She would never have allowed any harm to come to you. Perhaps if she knows that I spared your life, she will be grateful.'

Faro said nothing. He had no emotions to spare for a lovesick Colonel who had sacrificed a family life for a useless infatuation for the Grand Duchess Amelie of Luxoria.

The Colonel was looking at him wistfully, obviously hoping for a consoling response but all that Faro could say was, 'I don't think one should mistake gratitude for love or that any man would want a wife on such conditions.'

There were more urgent matters on Faro's mind. 'And the Kaiser? Did he know?'

The Colonel shrugged. 'I think not. But perhaps he suspected something was in the wind and that was why he diplomatically absented himself. He seemed anxious not to meet you, Mr Faro. I know him well and this is not quite in character, especially since you are a close and trusted servant of his beloved grandmother.'

By whose orders he had been instructed to return George to Luxoria, Faro thought coldly. He was beginning to suspect everyone in this plan to dispose of him, even Her Majesty the Queen.

The Colonel was saying, 'Wilhelm has no reason to hate you, unlike myself. As my rival for Amelie's affections, you have long been the unknown man who stood between us and I have hated your image and would gladly have you dead. But if I destroyed you it would not make Amelie love me and I never give up hope that someday she may.'

He smiled sadly. 'And then I did not know you, but now we have met and I have put a face and body on this hated rival. Then there is George, whom I love like my own son. In Amelie's many difficult times, when she has sought refuge here, I have felt that I stood *in loco parentis*. I was in a quandary. I could see the boy had formed an affection for you, as well as my nephew Anton. You had saved their lives.'

He spread his hands wide. 'But what could I do? The arrangement had already been made.'

And Faro remembered the scene he had witnessed, the brief tense words between the Colonel and Dieter as the latter apparently departed with the train to Luxoria.

'Dieter was to return, make his way to Mosheim and kill you. I could not do it myself, although I have killed of necessity in battle, I have never taken any man's life dishonourably. But Dieter is a hired assassin. It is merely another job of work with him.'

Leaning across, he put a hand on Faro's arm. 'But you are safe now, Mr Faro. You have my word as an officer and a gentleman. Now perhaps I can help you into these – ' he indicated a shirt and jacket on the chair nearby.

'Another new suit,' said Faro wryly.

'There are wardrobes of them here in the hunting-lodge, as I told you. Besides, those ones were required elsewhere,' he added grimly.

At Faro's puzzled glance he continued. 'There is a mill-race you will remember passing on the way up to the old woodcutter's cottage. By now it will have received Dieter's body in your clothes. By the time it is recovered, it will be unrecognisable as the policeman from Edinburgh. And President Gustav will be satisfied, having received secret information that his orders were carried out.'

'What of Dieter – won't he be expected to return to Luxoria, now that he is no longer needed as Anton's bodyguard?'

The Colonel shrugged. 'Dieter would not be welcome. He failed in his mission to return Anton to his father and to eliminate George. His services are expendable and since it is in the nature of hired killers to come and go without anyone expecting explanations, no awkward questions will be asked.'

And with a swift change of subject, he leaned forward and held up the shirt. 'But this, I am afraid, is going to be awkward – and painful.'

It was.

When the last button was fastened, a tap on the door announced George and Anton.

George rushed over to him. 'Are you all right, sir? We were on the archery course waiting for Mama to arrive.'

Faro glanced in the Colonel's direction, who shook his head. Amelie waiting to receive him in the woodcutter's hut had been part of the well-laid trap.

'We heard the shots and decided to have a look, especially as there isn't supposed to be any shooting up there,' said Anton.

'You must come and see our archery course and my falcon,' said George eagerly. Then looking across at the Colonel, 'Mama is waiting to see Mr Faro, Uncle Karl.' And to Faro, 'She heard that Anton's horse had thrown you. Please don't tell her what really happened. She might be frightened.'

'I cannot believe it,' said Anton. 'Dieter must have gone mad to have attacked you like that, Mr Faro. And after saving all our lives, too.'

Faro could think of no answer suitable for the boys. 'I was very thankful that your uncle arrived in time,' he said with a grateful smile in the Colonel's direction.

'It was dreadful,' said Anton. 'I had never seen anyone really dead before, Mr Faro. Just pretend in plays.'

'It was just like one of the adventure stories they try to keep from us at Glenatholl. But this was real blood,' said George with a shiver.

'Where is your Mama waiting?' the Colonel put in quickly.

'In the salon. She is not allowed to climb stairs until she is properly well again.' And remembering Faro's accident, 'Can you walk, sir, if we help you?'

'You're very kind, George, but I think I can manage. It's my ribs that are cracked, my legs are fine.' And he added to himself, 'somewhat shaky though to find I am still in one piece.'

When they reached the room where Amelie waited, the Colonel said to George, 'Your mother wishes to talk to Mr Faro alone.'

'Very well, sir,' said George, sounding a little disappointed and looking at Faro as if he did not wish to let him out of his sight.

'You must tell her all that has happened, Mr Faro, since we left Glenatholl. She will want to hear all the details. Leave nothing out. Everything – remember!'

Not quite everything, thought Faro. There were some things George must never know.

29

As he entered the room, Amelie looked up from the sofa where she was sitting. This time there was no formality. She indicated a place beside her and took his hand.

'My dear, I am so sorry. Karl tells me you had an accident with Anton's horse and you have cracked ribs. Is it very painful?'

Faro smiled bravely and she went on, 'What a terrible thing to happen when you have just arrived. The boys' mounts are chosen for their reliability. Something must have scared your horse.'

Faro decided to go along with this version of his accident. 'The animal wasn't to blame. I lost my stirrups. I'm afraid it is a long time since I was on a horse,' he said truthfully. 'There wasn't much call for it in my particular line of business.'

Touching his shoulder and assured that it didn't hurt, which wasn't entirely true, Amelie smiled and said, 'Dear Jeremy, I don't know where to begin. I owe you so much. But first of all, and most important, thank you again for bringing George home safe to me.'

Pausing, she looked into his face intently, as if memorising every feature. 'I can hardly believe you are here with me. I am scared to close my eyes in case I open them and you have disappeared,' she smiled sadly, 'as so often happens in my dreams. Now you are really here and I wonder if you can guess how many days of my life I have dreamed of this moment,' she whispered, patting the sofa. 'Of sitting here like this together and sharing an hour with the man who saved my life so long ago.'

As he began to protest she said in a low voice, as if they might be overheard, 'It is true, Jeremy. If George had not been born then I would never have survived Gustav's determined attempts on my life. But all that is past now.'

Closing her eyes, she sighed deeply. 'Now I can pretend for one perfect hour that I am not a Grand Duchess, but merely an ordinary housewife.' A wistful smile, 'Perhaps an Edinburgh policeman's wife and we are spending a holiday together travelling in Europe.'

Faro hadn't the heart to tell her that such things were beyond ordinary Edinburgh housewives, especially those on a policeman's salary.

Lifting his hand, she held it against her cheek. 'I can hardly believe that you are so unchanged by the years. Sometimes I have tried to remember your face and found I could not do so. That worried me; you meant so much to me and yet I had forgotten what you looked like. I could no longer bring your face to mind, as if I had an image of you that had faded away.'

Guiltily Faro recognised this experience as similar to his own, but for a vastly different reason – a deliberate attempt to eradicate all memory of that brief fateful visit of the Grand Duchess Amelie.

'There has not been a day in my life when I have not thought of you in the past thirteen years, Jeremy. Thinking what time it would be in Scotland and what you might be doing at that moment. And all the time railing against my destiny.'

Again that deep searching gaze into his face.

'Always saying if only – if only I had not been born a Grand Duchess, I could have made all my dreams come true. I could have been with you forever.'

And Faro listened sadly, wishing for her sake that he had been in love and that he could honestly share her emotions. Wishing he could say just once that it had been the same for him. For that was what she expected, as her right.

But it had never been so. Would it have been different if she had not been royal? Had some caution reasoned against loving someone far above him? Just as she must have always known that to love an Edinburgh policeman was a waste of time.

Acceptance had been easy for him. He had never loved her. That night of madness and passion long ago had never seemed part of his real life. Yet it had resulted in a child, ironically a now beloved son he could never claim as his own.

'I have talked to the Colonel,' he said trying desperately to get the conversation on to less emotional ground. 'I am glad you have such a friend.'

She sighed. 'I expect he told you that he loves me. Everyone knows about that. Such a good kind man, a great friend, but how could a Grand Duchess marry a mere Count?'

Or a policeman, thought Faro. What an intolerable existence it would have been. To be passionately in love – at the beginning – believing he could spend the rest of his life in her shadow in Luxoria. How love would have soon faded, changed into resentment.

'I have had one consolation through the years,' Amelie said, 'when I look at George. And he grows more like you every day. So I have always had a part of you, a mirror in him.' She sighed deeply. 'I would not mind dying now.'

'You must not talk of dying, Amelie. You have much to live for.'

She shook her head. 'Not now that I have seen you again. I have often thought I would give the rest of my life for one more hour together. Maybe God has been good and heard my prayer,' she whispered.

And Faro remembered the bullet that had lodged close to her heart and the odds on her survival, as she added, 'The future of

Luxoria is settled. That was why I came here to Mosheim this time, to make the final arrangements. Willy is to take care of everything.'

'What of President Gustav?'

She shrugged. 'He will be helpless against the might of Imperial Germany. And I have Willy's assurance that he will take good care of my people. I trust him, for he is a man of his word. Once, when we were in Balmoral, his uncle the Prince of Wales said that William the Great, as he called him, needed to learn that he is living near the end of the nineteenth century and not in the Middle Ages. Willy never forgot that. He was determined to prove him wrong. He did not care for his uncle, a feeling that was reciprocated.'

'How will your own people react to this annexation?'

'Agreeably, I think. They love me, they hate Gustav. They will believe that anything I choose for them is the right thing. Luxoria is a poor country, bled by his indulgence and extravagance. With Willy she will blossom and live again, share a new economy.'

She smiled. 'My people like him very much, you know, and they will learn to trust him. He has visited Luxoria many times, as my old friend, purely social visits. Willy is so popular with the people, a charming man – do you know they turned out in their thousands to watch his carriage pass by, to cheer him. How Gustav hated that!'

'And what of George's future in all this?'

'That is all decided. Willy will take care of his education until he is old enough for his official role.'

'But by then Luxoria will be part of Germany,' Faro reminded her gently. 'So it will be in name only, surely?'

'I do not think George will mind in the least. He has never cared for the prospect of ruling a country. He seems to have inherited other ideas of what he wants to do with his life.'

Faro let that pass as Amelie went on, 'Please tell my dear godmother when you return to Scotland that I leave my little country in her grandson's excellent keeping.'

Faro knew the chances were remote indeed that he would be able to approach Her Majesty with such a message.

'Your Queen will be pleased with our decision,' Amelie continued, 'because that was what her beloved Prince Albert, my very dear uncle, always wanted for Prussia.'

A clock struck the hour, slowly, solemnly.

Amelie sighed. 'If only . . . if only. Are they the cruelest words in any language? Soon it will be time for you to leave. For us to part,' she looked at him calmly, candidly. 'I think we are unlikely ever to meet again.'

She leaned forward and kissed Faro on the mouth. He held her close, briefly, wishing he could say and mean the words she longed to hear.

'This is our real parting, dearest Jeremy,' she whispered. 'Our official one will be, alas, much more formal. But there is someone else I want you to meet, if you would – ' she indicated the bell-pull.

A moment later the door opened to admit a vision of elegance, a large-eyed, large-bosomed woman, swept dramatically into the room, looking as if she had just stepped off the stage. She ran swiftly to Amelie and kissed her. Anton was close behind his mother, their likeness immediate.

She had not seen Faro and following Amelie's whisper, turned to face him.

Amelie smiled. 'This is Melissa, Karl's sister.'

And Gustav's late mistress, thought Faro, as the vision bore down upon him.

'So you are – ' her eyes widened as she turned and looked at Amelie. Then she laughed, a deep-throated laugh. 'How could anyone be mistaken?' She wagged a finger at him. 'I have heard all about you, Monsieur Faro and there is someone here dying to see you.'

She called out, 'Enter!' and the door opened to admit another woman, tall, slender, auburn-haired, green-eyed. And in Faro's eyes, the most beautiful woman in the world.

'Imogen!' he gasped. 'What on earth are you doing here?' he

asked, holding her hand formally but longing to gather her into his arms.

Laughing, she indicated the woman talking to Amelie. 'That's Lisa, the opera singer friend I told you about.'

'Such a small world!'

'Sure now, isn't it just? Too small for comfort sometimes. Too small for secrets too.'

Faro ignored that arch smile, as she looked at him searchingly. 'Well now, Faro. And what have you been doing to yourself? I hear you have cracked ribs.'

'Trouble with a horse,' he murmured.

Imogen laughed. 'Life is full of surprises, Faro. All this time and you never even told me you could ride a horse. Not one of your accomplishments you've ever cared to discuss with me, like some others that are now seeing the light of day.'

Ignoring her teasing smile, Faro said, 'But what are you doing in Mosheim?'

'I came with Lisa. We've been in Munich and are on our way back to Heidelberg. She wanted me to meet Amelie, who I understand loves Scotland and had a very interesting holiday there once, about thirteen years ago. That was before we met, of course,' she added primly.

If she expected a reply to that, she wasn't getting one.

'Amelie talks of nothing else to Lisa,' she went on with a sideways glance over at the diva. 'Lisa is leaving immediately, she's singing Beethoven's *Fidelio* in Heidelberg. This is just a fleeting visit.' She paused, looking at the little group chattering, oblivious of their presence. 'I can go with her if you're planning to stay on for a while.'

'No!' said Faro sharply. 'I'm not staying.' He took her hand. 'I want – desperately – just to be with you again. To have you all to myself and that means without Lisa. The Colonel was to send you a telegraph at Heidelberg – that I had arrived.'

That pleased her. 'And me not even there. A good thing your

plans were delayed.' She looked at him impishly and nodded towards the door. 'The other lad is waiting for you. I saw him as I came in. Said he wanted a word.'

In answer Faro went over to Amelie and Melissa, bowed and held out his hand. 'Goodbye, Amelie.'

He hoped she was not going to cry for her voice trembled as she said, 'Please see George before you go.'

Melissa took his hand in a strong grip. 'You are not really going to leave us so soon, Mr Faro,' she whispered. Her eyelids fluttered seductively. 'We have only just met.'

Faro bowed. 'I hope to see you again – in *Fidelio.*'

George was waiting for him. 'Mama said you must go. That you couldn't stay for a while.' He had none of his mother's restraint, none of that adult world of dissembling had touched his childish sorrow at losing Faro.

'It's so unfair.' And putting his thin arms around Faro he sobbed. 'You should have been my father. You who are so good and true, not that – that – beast, who ill-used my mother, and Anton's mother too. I hate him and would give everything in the world to call you father, to say that word just once.'

It was said, it hung in the air between them. Too late Faro's hand covered gently the boy's mouth. 'No, Highness, no,' he whispered. 'You – we – must never think about it.'

And George threw his arms around Faro again. 'It is you I will love as a father, your image I shall carry when I'm a man. You, I will try to be like. I want so much for you to be proud of me.'

'That I am, George. And will always be,' said Faro as he hugged the boy to him, stroked his cheek then gently released him. And he thought that the pain in his heart at this parting was greater than any physical agony he had ever suffered.

'We will meet again – some day. Promise!' George whispered.

'No, lad. I can't promise you that, but I can promise I'll never forget the bravest prince that ever lived.'

'May I write to you, then?' George asked, fighting back the tears.

'Of course. I would be honoured. Goodbye, lad.'

'Goodbye – ' and the word, the ever-forbidden word followed him in a whisper. But Faro heard it.

Imogen was waiting for him outside, his battered valise at her feet. As they walked into the winter sunshine, she took his arm, aware that his emotions were running high, that this man who rarely wept was very close to it now.

'That's a fine young lad. We had a chat. A very interesting encounter. Do you know, he reminds me very much of someone – ' she added archly. 'If only I could think who – or, more important, when and why.'

Faro looked at her sharply, wondering how much she had guessed or been told by Lisa who was Amelie's confidant.

She squeezed his hand gently, stood on tiptoe and kissed his cheek. 'I'm glad I came and met Amelie at last.'

It was a sign. She knew. But his secret was safe with her. She knew her own place in his life was unchallenged and would remain so.

'You must tell me all about your adventures. All of them, I mean. Leave nothing out,' she laughed.

'Sometime – maybe,' he said wearily.

She smiled up at him. 'Whither now, Faro?'

'Whither indeed. I wish I knew. Meanwhile, I think the next train to Heidelberg.'

And the two, both exiles of a sort, walked arm in arm towards the waiting carriage.